# By instinct Maitland stepped into the dark shadow of the trees

Before him, in a tangled wilderness of shrubs frosted by moonlight, lay the rumored haunt of the witch coven. Suddenly he stiffened. Had he heard it— a whispered voice, the catch of a breath? Some local lover and his lass?

But it was an unlikely night for a dalliance.

Then he felt, rather than heard, the sound of stealthy movement behind him, and was suddenly gripped by the terrible fear of nighttime imaginings...and the sharp pervasive smell of danger!

# Keeping you in suspense is our business

RAVEN HOUSE takes pride in having
its name added to the select
list of prestigious publishers
that have brought—in the
nearly one and one-half centuries
since the appearance of the
first detective story—the finest
examples of this exciting
literary form to millions of readers
around the world.

Edgar Allan Poe's
*The Murders in the Rue Morgue*
started it all in 1841.
We at RAVEN HOUSE are proud
to continue the tradition.

**Raven House Mysteries**

*Let us keep you in suspense.*

# THEY LOVE NOT POISON

**Sara Woods**

A RAVEN HOUSE MYSTERY FROM
# W🌐RLDWIDE
TORONTO •LONDON• NEW YORK • SYDNEY

The events described in this story
took place in January 1947.

S.W.

———————————————•-•-•———————————————

Raven House edition published January 1982

Second printing January 1982

ISBN 0-373-63020-4

# 1

HE CROSSED THE RIVER at Riddingstones and stopped when he was halfway over to admire the swirl of water against the polished rock, and think how unpleasant it would be to get a ducking on so cold a night. It would have been more sensible to return by the packhorse bridge, a mile or so upstream, but when he passed it he had stayed by instinct in the shadow of the trees. The truth was he had still been in the grip of fear, and concerned only to put as much distance as he could between himself and How Gill.

Now that the thought was formulated he allowed himself to dwell on it as he completed the crossing and set off up the path that led past the Claytons' cottage to join Stavethorpe Edge just opposite the Hall. Let's face it, he told himself, I was afraid, as scared as any schoolgirl making her way to bed after an evening of ghost stories. But—much as he would have liked to believe it—he knew that came nowhere near the truth. What had worried him had been a much more immediate and familiar sensation than any nighttime imagining. The smell of danger. . . .

What then had reminded him? The whispering voices, the catching of breath, the sudden, deadly silence, and then the sense, rather than the sound, of stealthy movement. Some local lover and his lass? He grinned at the thought, though the grin had a twist of bitterness in it, because it was an unlikely

night for dalliance even though the moon was high
and serene. He could see the stile quite clearly as he
came up to it, and the road white beyond, and then
his attention was taken by a pair of headlights,
sweeping around the bend. Not a new car, it was
making heavy weather of the steepest part of the
hill, and turning into the gate of Stavethorpe
Hall... an odd time of night, surely, for visiting? Or
perhaps the Thorntons were having a party. He
saw, without much interest, that there was a car
already drawn up on the gravel sweep before the
house.

He set off at a steady pace up the hill. A useful
piece of gossip to retail when he got back to the
farm. He would go in quite casually, and they
would think only that he had walked off the restlessness a day's reading had engendered. Because
one thing was certain, he wasn't going to tell them
what he had heard—what he had thought he
heard—in How Gill. Bill would laugh and pretend to
believe he had stopped in at the Pennypot on his
way and had one too many, and Jenny would look
at him with the quick flare of anxiety in her eyes
that she never had, and perhaps never would, put
in words. And both of them would think, *he'll get
over it—got to make allowances,* and then, inevitably, *only his imagination....*

The trouble was, how could he be sure they
wouldn't be right?

Bill Cleveland had been demobilized from the air
force a year ago and had bought the farm that was
called Brass Castle, with ninety-three acres, at the
auction in Great Allerton some three months later.
Not easy land, hard and uncompromising, on the
very edge of the moor, but the house was sheltered
from the north in the lee of the hill and looked out
across Thorburndale—the best view in England, or
so Bill said. Antony and Jenny Maitland had come

for Christmas, and somehow the visit had been pro-
longed. Antony was reading for the bar and found
the exercise no more difficult here than in London,
while Jenny had thrown herself with her usual enthusiasm into all the activities of the farm. She and
Bill had been sitting by the fire when he left, pleasantly somnolent after a day in the open. Neither of
them had offered to accompany him; perhaps they
had sensed that he wanted to be alone. The life he
had led during the war years did not make it easy to
settle down now to the concentrated course of
study that was necessary if he still wished to follow
his chosen career; it was only stubbornness—which,
he reflected wryly, must be regarded as a flaw in
his character, not a virtue—that kept him to his
books at all.

The top of the hill. When he turned to look back
across the darkened valley, even the lights of Stavethorpe Hall were out of sight. Ram's Syke on his
right, a wilderness of tough ling and boulders, frosted in the moonlight; turn left, then along High
Lane. A moment later he was pulling open the
heavy gate that led to the track to the farm, a stony
track that was said to date from the Iron Age—and
perhaps that was true, because it plunged down the
hill between steep banks that were more than head
high. Here, if anywhere, should be the ghosts, the
long forgotten men and women who had made their
way from Wharfedale and Washburndale to cross
the Thorburn at Dallow Bridge and lose their breath
on the hillside beyond.

There had been a night not so many years ago, or
so very far from here, when he had been out on the
moor through all the dark hours. . . waiting. Then it
had been April, and too cold for comfort, but there
had been the scent of spring in the air. Now the
earth was dead, iron-bound in frost, and still. . . ut-
terly still. Only when he came near the farm build-

ings there was a rustle of straw and a quiet grunt-
ing sound; one of the sows talking in her sleep,
most likely. And when he passed the barn there
was the fragrance of clover-sweet hay, and then
the tang of wood smoke from the farmhouse chim-
ney.

The front door, which was heavy and nail studded—"useful if we ever want to fortify the place,"
as Bill had pointed out—led directly into the living
room, which was stone flagged, with cream-washed
walls, and had a great open fireplace in which some
odd pieces of planking were blazing merrily. There
was Jenny, her brown curls gilded in the lamplight,
turning her head to smile at him; and there was Bill,
stretched out at the other side of the hearth, raising
a hand in lazy salute. Antony was conscious, for an
instant only, of a feeling that was almost resentment. Bill had been a bomber pilot, and shot down
twice: once over the sea, and once over occupied
France. But now he was as relaxed as if he had
never known any other way of life than farming,
and slept easily at night, while Antony himself. . . .
He closed the door carefully behind him, resisting
the impulse to leave it standing open, and came
across to the fire.

"Did you have a good walk?"

"Yes, thank you." He had thrown his gloves and
muffler onto a chair as he came in, and now he
stretched his hands to the blaze, not looking at
either of his companions. "There seem to be visitors
at Stavethorpe Hall."

"The doctor, most likely."

"Oh?" The right note of casual inquiry. Nothing
to show—surely—that anything had disturbed him.

"Mrs. Thornton is dead."

Antony turned his head at that. "But you know
the Thorntons," he said, as though this made the
whole idea preposterous.

"That's no guarantee of their immortality." Bill sounded amused.

"No, of course not. But how did you happen to hear?"

"They sent for Mrs. Dibb."

"Is she a nurse?" He still sounded incredulous, this time, perhaps, with better cause.

"What would they want a nurse for...now?" asked Bill reasonably.

"I thought—"

"Mrs. Dibb is always sent for when somebody in the district dies; she lays them out."

"I see," said Antony blankly. He did not sound as if this was true. "You're pretty casual about it," he added. "I thought they were friends of yours."

"Cyril is," said Bill, heaving himself up a little from his lounging position. "And so is Bess, of course. But I shan't shed any tears for Hester; she was a shrew."

"I don't suppose you ought to say that now," said Jenny lazily. Antony looked down and smiled at her and was aware, with a slight sinking of his spirits, that her answering look held something of inquiry.

"You're as heartless as Bill is," he told her. He thought perhaps he was laboring the subject, but he went on anyway. "It didn't sound like a doctor's car, or look like one, for that matter. It was old—"

"They most of them are, these days," said Bill.

"Not so old as this. One of those very upright cars that always look as if Queen Mary was sitting bolt upright on the back seat. There was a tin trunk on the luggage grid—"

"Was there, though? That sounds like Sergeant Newbould."

"What on earth does he use it for?"

"The local theory is that it's, to keep clues in. What I don't see is what he was doing there."

"In a case of sudden death—" said Antony vaguely, and waved a hand to show that he did not mean to finish the sentence.

"Not so sudden, really. She's been suffering from some sort of gastric trouble for several months now."

"Tell me about the Thorntons." He turned to survey the fire. "How are we for wood? Can I use some of this?"

"All you want. I can get some more tomorrow."

"What luxury." He looked rather doubtfully at the piece of timber in his hand. "We aren't burning the old homestead, are we? I shouldn't like to think—"

"It's the stalls from the long barn," Jenny told him. "Bill wants them burned."

"In that case—" He threw the wood on the fire and watched idly as it began to spit and crackle. "Tell me about the Thorntons," he said again without turning his head.

"There's nothing to tell. They're the most ordinary people imaginable."

"I didn't think you found—"

"He's a gentleman farmer," said Jenny, interrupting rather quickly. "Whatever that means. Norman says more gentleman than farmer."

"I didn't know Norman had it in him to be so uncharitable."

"He likes people who work hard," said Bill rather smugly. "That's the only reason he condescends to work for me."

"How very unnerving. Suppose you want to take a holiday."

"That would be all right, I think, providing he felt I'd earned it. That's one thing about living in this part of the world—it does keep you up to the mark," said Bill. He was a large young man with smooth, dark hair and a square, unemotional face, and in spite of the fact that he was wearing an old pullover with a darn at the elbow and a pair of gray flannel trousers that must have been left over from his prewar wardrobe, he contrived to look as though he had never done a day's work in his life. Antony was tall, too, and dark, but that was about the only resemblance between them. "Anyway," Bill went on, "Cyril's a nice chap, whether Norman approves of him or not. And—if Jenny will allow me to speak ill of the dead for two seconds only—Hester was the world's worst termagant and he was extraordinarily patient with her. I think he'd have liked a family, but whether she couldn't or wouldn't I don't know."

That was treading on dangerous ground, though Bill couldn't know it, and it was Antony's turn to speak rather hastily into the silence, forgetting his own uneasiness and saying the first thing that came into his head. "How many acres has he?"

"About two hundred in hand. And he owns a couple of farms out on the Beckwith road. Marginal land; I don't suppose he gets much in the way of rent from them."

"What about the girl?"

"Bess? She isn't a Thornton, her name's Foster."

"But she's living at Stavethorpe Hall, isn't she? I thought you said—"

"That's right. She's Hester's cousin. More like a niece, really; she's so much younger."

"A nice girl?" Antony persisted, ignoring the fact that Jenny was pulling a face at him.

"Nice enough," said Bill. And before Antony could ask any more questions, the door behind the staircase opened and Mrs. Dibb came in.

Mrs. Dibb was Bill's housekeeper—a large, placid person, very like her son, Norman, who worked on the farm and also lived in the house. "I brought your cocoa," she announced. The tray went down on the sideboard with a thump. "Sit down, Mr.

Maitland, like a Christian, and drink it while it's hot. It will warm you up."

Antony accepted the cup and said, "Thank you," quite meekly.

Bill said, "I didn't think you'd be back so quickly. How did you manage it?"

And Jenny said, "Perhaps it wasn't true. Perhaps Mrs. Thornton wasn't really dead." Mrs. Dibb smiled at her—people usually did smile at Jenny—but it was to Bill that she spoke.

"Seems they didn't want me after all. That Constable Lister, he said they had it all in hand. Taking her to Great Allerton, that's what they were doing."

"Why on earth did they want to do a thing like that?"

"Inquest," said Antony. He had seated himself obediently, but his eyes were on the housekeeper's face. "A formality," he said. "No more than that."

"Well, I don't know, Mr. Maitland. Not but what I expect you'd know about things like that, along of your books and all. But there was Dr. Todd, and seemingly he wouldn't sign t'certificate. Well, he has to do what he thinks is right. And there was Mr. Thornton, looking as if he was dazed, poor man, and Miss Foster tired right out. I told her to go straight to bed. She was up all last night, you see, Mrs. Thornton having been took bad sometime yesterday evening."

"I didn't realize that."

"Well, Mr. Cleveland, there's got to be some things as aren't revealed to us." This sounded uncommonly like an apology; certainly there wasn't much that went on in the neighborhood that didn't come to Mrs. Dibb's ears one way or another. "So they'll have a coroner's inquest, if that's what they want, and I don't know as anyone'll be any the better off for it. Worse off, if you ask me; there's been too much talk already."

"What sort of talk?" asked Bill, rather more sharply than was his custom.

But Mrs. Dibb seemed already to have regretted having spoken. "*Wicked* talk," she said, and closed her mouth with a snap on the words, as though to indicate that the subject was closed.

"Who—?"

"You'd best drink your cocoa, all of you," said Mrs. Dibb in an admonitory tone. "It's getting late." She paused a moment as though waiting for any signs of mutiny, and then went out, closing the door firmly behind her.

There was a moment's silence. Jenny was sipping her cocoa, looking at Bill thoughtfully over the rim of the cup. Antony had got to his feet again, and was kicking the fire into a blaze. Bill said resignedly, "It's never any good asking her questions if she doesn't want to answer them."

"All the same, I wonder what she meant," said Antony, turning to stand with his back to the grate. He was feeling warm and relaxed now, and could almost have believed that when he passed through How Gill his imagination had been at work; only the faintest thread of uneasiness stayed stubbornly at the back of his mind.

"Anything...nothing. Oh, to hell with it," said Bill with uncharacteristic violence. "There's always talk in the country."

"*Wicked* talk." Unconsciously Antony echoed the housekeeper's tone. Jenny put down her cup.

"I don't think it would really take much to shock her, you know."

"Don't you think so?" asked Antony skeptically.

"She's always lived here, hasn't she? In Thorburndale."

"You can see more of life in the country—"

Bill didn't seem to have been listening. "I'll go to

see Cyril tomorrow,'' he said, obviously unconscious that he was interrupting. And now it seemed
as if he couldn't leave the subject alone. They were
still discussing it ten minutes later when they separated for the night.

II

"I CAN'T SEE WHY he was so worried,'' said Antony
when he and Jenny were alone together, if you
could call it alone with the Valor Perfection stove
standing companionably in the corner and sending
its shadows darting and flickering around the
room.... Antony always maintained that its pres-
ence made him self-conscious. "It isn't as if he was
in love with the girl,'' he said now, and sounded
more positive than he felt.

"Isn't he?''

"I thought so once. I thought we'd got him off at
last. But now I think I was wrong.''

"Why?'' asked Jenny, who was brushing her hair.
The one candle in the red kitchen candlestick stood
out of the way on the bedside table, and in the dim
light her face looked back at her from the mirror,
shadowed and unfamiliar.

"He had every excuse to talk about her tonight,
but I didn't think he sounded particularly enthusiastic.''

"He said she was 'nice enough.' That's practically
a eulogy, coming from Bill.''

"Come now, he isn't a Yorkshireman,'' Antony
protested.

"The more I see of Mrs. Dibb and Norman, the
more I think he ought to be,'' said Jenny, who had
known Bill as long as she could remember. "Anyway, you shouldn't tease him.''

"If you call it teasing—''

"I do.''

"It's only simple politeness to show an interest—" He broke off and came across the room to stand behind her, and grinned when he met her eyes in the mirror. "She sounds all right to me."

"Of course, she is rather young," said Jenny with the air of one making a concession. "Not quite twenty, Bill says."

"Considering that we were married when you were eighteen—"

"That's quite different. You're three years older than I am, and that was almost exactly four years ago, and Bill's older than you are *now*."

"Not one of your more lucid statements, Jenny. Bill is precisely seven months older than I am; that isn't subject to change, as far as I know."

"You know quite well what I mean."

"You mean that Bill is seven years older than Bess Foster. I don't see that it matters at all."

"Of course it doesn't," said Jenny, changing sides again. She put down the hairbrush, grimaced at her reflection, and then turned so that she could look up at him directly. "Antony—"

"Well?"

The momentary hesitation had spoiled the casualness of the question. "Did you enjoy your walk?"

"Very much indeed."

His mind is closed against me, she thought, or perhaps it was only the effect of the uncertain light, giving his face a set and stubborn look. "Did you meet anyone?" she asked.

"Not a soul." The simple truth, and for some reason it sounded like a lie. "I wouldn't expect to on so cold a night. Anyway, country people don't walk for fun."

"No, I suppose not."

Leave it there. "Why?" he asked in his turn, and surprised himself with the question. Then, because she looked at him blankly, "Why do you ask?"

"I just wondered." Obviously she had no intention of completing the sentence. She got up purposefully, and went across to struggle with the window, which was inclined to stick. When she had finished, and Antony had propped it open, she seemed to have forgotten her query; but Antony, lying awake later in the darkness, wondered if she was awake, too, and did not ask.

**2**

THE NIGHT SEEMED to have done nothing to calm his restlessness, and the sight of his books, piled untidily on the table in the little room Bill had made into an office, gave him a feeling of sharp distaste. He went to the window first—a small, mullioned window set in a wall that was all of three feet thick—but there was nothing much to be seen from here; just the garth behind the house where the breeding sows had their run, with a solitary pig digging a hole, quietly but intently, as though it might be conducting some sort of scientific experiment.

Mrs. Dibb had laid the fire, but as long as he didn't put a match to it he wasn't committed to staying indoors. He went upstairs instead to find the heavy woolen sweater that Jenny, in a fit of domesticity, had knitted for him during the war. The bed had been made already, the white counterpane was smooth and unwrinkled, and the room had been tidied. There was a new candle in the red candlestick and a new box of matches with the picture of a tiger on it; he remembered now that he had used the last of the old ones last night. He wasn't sure how good Jenny was at household details; all their married life had been lived in his uncle's house . . . if you could call it living when he had been away so much. It might be a natural efficiency asserting itself, it might be Mrs. Dibb's influence. He'd find out soon enough, he supposed, when the alterations to the house in Kempenfeldt Square were finished, and they had their own flat on the top floor.

When he got downstairs again, his gloves and scarf had gone from the chair inside the front door, but he found them, with his jacket, in the cupboard by the kitchen entrance. The kitchen was warm enough to tempt him to linger: a big room with an open-fire range, a rag rug on the flags in front of it, and a ham and half a side of bacon hanging from the rafters. The fire was made up with coke that Bill had fetched himself in the trailer from Great Allerton, because the coal ration didn't really go very far and had to be saved for baking days. There were a couple of easy chairs, one with a cushion in the seat, as though it had sagged too far for comfort; a table with a well-scrubbed top; a set of ladder-back dining chairs; and an old-fashioned dresser with a confused medley of crockery—the best that Bill had been able to beg, borrow or steal from his family, most likely, and lucky to have that. There wasn't anything new to be bought in the shops—he and Jenny had tried it—except export rejects, and they were scarce enough.

He could hear voices from the scullery, and when he put his head around the door, there, sure enough, were Jenny and Mrs. Dibb washing up the breakfast dishes. "It's too nice a morning to stay in," he said. "Would you like a walk, Jenny?"

"You go along, luv," said Mrs. Dibb. "It'll do you good."

"Well, in a minute, Antony. When we've finished."

"You'll find me outside, then, talking to Bill."

He went out by the kitchen door and turned right along the front of the house toward the piggeries. He found Bill mucking out one of the sties, while the occupant, a large white sow with eleven sturdy piglets at her heels, ran briskly around the lower garth. It was a fine, clear day . . . fine and very cold. "What I call a hundred-pound day," said Bill, heaving a last forkful of soiled straw into the wheelbarrow, and taking up a spade to snap the wire on a new bale.

"Cheap at the price, I'd say. But why?"

"When I first looked over the place I fixed in my mind the amount I'd go to at the auction. It was more than I could afford, at that. But that was on a gray day; then I came up for another look around on a morning like this and promptly raised the limit."

"Did you need to use the extra hundred quid?"

"Yes, I did. I was lucky, really, to get it at all."

"Were there many people after it?" He hadn't meant to sound disbelieving, having fallen in love with Brass Castle himself at first sight, but for him it was a refuge only, something outside the normal stream of living, which sooner or later, he realized, must be entered upon again.

Bill was shaking out the fresh straw into a bed at the back of the sty. "More than I expected," he said. "Cyril Thornton was bidding, but he fell out quite early on. I didn't know him then, of course."

"Your neighbor at Stavethorpe Hall?"

"Yes. Jenny didn't like what I said last night about Hester, but it was true enough. *And* she was stingy. Cyril said to me later, 'If I'd had Hester's backing I'd at least have given you a run for your money.' That was the nearest he ever came to criticizing her, and I admit it made me feel a bit awkward."

"I suppose it meant he wanted Brass Castle and she didn't."

"I suppose so."

"It also sounds as if she held the purse strings."

"That's not unusual in this part of the world. But in this case—" Bill sounded as if he would be glad enough to be rid of the subject now "—I've heard it was true in the sense you mean it."

"I see. Who else wanted Brass Castle?" asked Antony obligingly, and Bill answered with ill-disguised pleasure at the change of course.

"There was a farmer from Ellerdale; he was with me all the way, and if he'd bid once more I'd have been out of the running. I found out afterward he was one of Wilfred Damerel's tenants from Priest Monkton, and he was there as Damerel's agent. There must have been some misunderstanding between them, because I heard later that Damerel was furious not to have got the place. He wanted it for his son, Patrick. Something like that. And I don't think there'd be any question of his not being able to afford it."

"I've heard you speak of the Damerels before."

"Yes, they're a nice family, and I don't think Wilfred bears me any grudge for getting ahead of him. They live at Dallow Park, but they own land right over into Ellerdale—a lot of it's moor, of course."

The sow had come down from the garth, and was snuffling inquisitively in the door of her sty. Antony moved aside politely to let her pass. "How Gill is just upriver from Dallow Bridge, isn't it? Is there a house there?"

"On the far bank. . . Burntside Hall. The manager of the Great Allerton branch of the Northumbrian and Wessex Bank lives there . . . chap called Undercliffe. He looks after my overdraft for me, and I've met them here and there. He has a nice wife, but I don't really know them very well. The family is grown, I think, and away from home."

"As a resident of a mere nine months' standing you seem to have done pretty well getting to know your neighbors."

"They're a friendly lot. Look here, are you going for a walk?"

"When Jenny is ready."

"Wait for me, then." Pig and piglets were back in the sty now; he closed the door on them and adjusted a piece of sacking carefully over the peephole. "Got to look after the old girl," he said. "She's the best sow I've got and I want to build up my breeding stock from her."

"What's her name?"

"Her registered name is Ferrenscross Snowflake, but I call her Grunter, which seems more appropriate. At that, I sometimes think it ought to be Lady Macbeth."

"Why on earth?"

" '*Bring forth men children only.*' I bought her in pig, and she had a litter of twelve, but only two of them were gilts. This time there's only one."

"Gilts being. . .?"

"They're not called sows until they've had their first litter."

"I see." He watched Bill stoop to the handles of the wheelbarrow and followed him when he trundled it away toward the midden. "Did you say you were coming with us?"

"As far as Stavethorpe Hall. But I'll have to wash first, and get out of my overalls. Do you mind waiting?"

"You'll probably be ready before Jenny is, anyway." They started to walk back toward the house. "I'll stay out here and commune with nature. Or. . . where's Norman? There's nothing like watching other people work."

"In the dairy, I should think. Or in the mistal, if he's finished there. There's not much to be done at this time of year, you know."

"There's milking twice a day."

"But we only send away one churn. It's a sideline, really; the pigs are the thing."

"I rather like Buttercup and Bluebell and Daffodil. . . what I've seen of them."

"They're nice creatures," Bill agreed. "And it's really easier to take a churn up to the road than to fetch milk every day from one of our neighbors."

Bill went in, and Antony wandered on until he came to the mistal, where he found Laddie, the sheep dog, on guard in the doorway, and inside Norman in wordless communion with a heifer called, rather tactlessly, Cowslip. "Coming along nicely, she is," he said, and his big hands were gentle as he rubbed the cow's flank in a friendly way. "Ready for t'bull any day, I wouldn't wonder."

Norman was six foot five, and looked even taller in the heavy, wooden-soled clogs he wore. He was broad in proportion, though without an ounce of fat; and he could make his voice heard easily from three fields away, or he could roar you, thought Antony (whose mind was running on Shakespeare since Bill's quotation had directed it there), as 'twere any sucking dove. The confidence about Cowslip was a gesture of friendship, as he realized well enough, toward one whose way of life was so different from his own as to be incomprehensible; it might even be an indirect expression of sympathy, though that was something he would rather not think about. In either event, he must make some sort of response, so he said with a show of interest, being already fairly well versed in the ways of the farm, "Where do you take her?"

"Over to Winterscale. It's nobbut a step. But Mr. Micklefield has a nice young 'un that'll be ready for service soon. I'm thinking Mr. Cleveland might do worse than buy him."

It would be unkind to point out that Bill's greatest interest was in the pigs, when Norman's heart was so obviously in the cowshed. All five of its occupants had turned to look at him now, the three in milk and the two followers. Under their meditative stare Antony said weakly, "That sounds like a good idea," as though they could understand him just as well as Norman could and might be cheered by the thought of a treat in store, or depressed by the prospect of its withholding.

Norman said, "Aye," and he sounded thoughtful, too. He moved to the next stall and began to rub Hyacinth gently behind the ear. "You're an educated man, Mr. Maitland." It was a simple statement of fact, a tribute, perhaps, to the pile of books Antony had brought with him from London. "Do you believe in witches, and all like that?"

"I've never really thought about it." Nor had he ever considered, he realized now, the sort of questions that might occupy Norman's mind as he went about his work. "There were certainly people who practiced witchcraft; I daresay they believed in what they were doing. But whether they ever did any good by it—or any evil, I should say—I just don't know."

"There were folk who believed in it, I've heard. Clever men who wrote books."

"I suppose so."

"But I didn't mean in t'old days, any road. There are stories enough about that, though I don't say as they all are true."

He stopped there, and Antony, whose interest was caught by so unlikely a choice of subject, asked curiously, "What did you mean, then?"

"Do you believe in them now . . . today?"

"That's something else again." He thought about it for a while. Norman, who was never in a hurry, went on scratching Hyacinth's ear. "There was an account in one of the livelier newspapers a month or so ago about a coven that's supposed to be meeting somewhere in Suffolk, but I don't know whether it was true."

"Hereabouts they used to meet in How Gill." Norman's eyes on Antony's face were almost as rumi-

native as the cows'. "Sithee, Mr. Maitland, they say
it's happening again."

"Who say?"

"People. Mrs. Dodgson told mother—proper upset
she is about it, too, because they do say as Mrs.
Thornton—"

"Was a witch?" He managed not to smile at the
idea. Norman shook his head.

"Not that. No. They say there was something funny about her death."

"Surely that's nonsense."

Norman shrugged. "So I was wondering, Mr.
Maitland—" were they coming to the heart of the
matter now "—you were out walking again last
night."

"Certainly I was." He spoke more abruptly than
he had intended.

But Norman gave no sign that he noticed the acer-
bity of his tone, asking instead, in his slow way,
"Do you know what day it is?"

That took a little calculation. "Monday," said Antony. And then, after a moment, "The sixth of
January."

"The feast of the Epiphany," said Norman, surprising him.

"What of it?"

"They do say on t'night before a feast day—"

Antony laughed. His amusement was genuine,
but a little shamefaced, as well. If what had scared
him was nothing but a bunch of cranks. . . . "Surely
not at this time of year . . . in this weather."

"They say they don't feel t'cold."

"Well, I'm sorry. I was through How Gill last
night, but I didn't see or hear anything to prove or
disprove the theory." That, if not quite the truth,
was not quite a lie, either. "As for Mrs. Thornton's
death, I really don't think Mrs. Dibb need worry
about it." (Though it was funny, wasn't it, that a

police sergeant had been in attendance last night, if the car he saw really had been Sergeant New-bould's, as Bill believed.) He broke off as he heard a step on the cobbles outside. "There's Bill now. I was just waiting for him."

"I'd not say owt to Mr. Cleveland, think on."

"About the witches?"

"Nay, I meant about Mrs. Thornton. It might worry him, him and Mr. Thornton being friends and all."

"I see. No, of course I won't mention it." He raised a hand in farewell, and turned and went out into the yard. Jenny and Bill were waiting for him. They went through the gate into the field, and began to walk across the rough grass toward Stavethorpe Edge. Laddie, who was Norman's dog, waved his tail politely but stayed where he was near his master. The senior of the barn cats, generally known as Big Pussy—a name that was at the moment particularly apt—stalked across their path, intent on her own affairs.

The sun was bright, the sky brilliantly blue . . . an improbable blue, Antony thought, for anything but a Mediterranean postcard. The field gate let them out onto the Edge, a few yards below High Lane. As they turned down the hill there was the craggy outline of Ram's Syke on their left, the Brass Castle pasture on their right, and below them, as they came to the corner, a coppice of pine trees that had been planted about twenty years ago. Antony said with some amusement in his tone, "Did you know there's supposed to be a coven that meets in How Gill?"

"Who told you that?"

"Norman. Was he pulling my leg?"

Bill frowned. "That's very unlikely. But the story's unlikely, too."

"Well, is it? Country people have long memories."

"If it used to happen, they're quite capable of talking about it as if it were yesterday," Bill agreed.

"It would be interesting to know if there's any local history—"

Bill took him up a little too quickly. (Humoring me, thought Antony, more than a shade resentfully.) "You ought to talk to Arthur Micklefield about that. It's his hobby."

"Is he a neighbor, too?" asked Jenny, when Antony was silent.

"Yes. He and his wife live at Ferrenscross. He was a professor in the English department at Leeds University before he retired. He farms about a hundred and fifty acres. That's really a hobby, too; Seth Dodgson's his bailiff. But they're nice people."

"A ruddy lot of paragons," said Antony. It would have been difficult to tell whether there was still amusement in his tone, or whether he meant the remark to be taken seriously.

"Who are?"

"Your neighbors. . . according to you."

"Except for poor Mrs. Thornton," said Jenny, looking from one of them to the other.

"Yes, of course." He didn't want to think about Mrs. Thornton, or what Norman had said about her death. Which was ridiculous, really. . . as ridiculous as the fact that the whole subject of the witches made him uneasy. If he had said last night. . . if he could say even now, "I heard something when I was coming through How Gill"—but he couldn't, and that was that. He knew that Jenny was worried about him—his arm was out of the sling now, but there was nothing more to be done about his shoulder, the doctors said, except to hope that time might ease the pain a little; and he guessed that she had confided her worry to Bill. All the same, he was determined not to let the matter drop altogether, even if Bill did have the nerve to think it would do him good to find some subject that held his interest. "Do you suppose this Mr. Micklefield would mind if I went to see him?"

"I'll phone him at lunchtime. I expect he'd be very glad." They had rounded the second corner now, and the view had opened out again before them. "What else did Norman have to tell you?"

"He wants you to buy a bull."

Bill laughed. "If he had his way we'd be milking a couple of dozen, and that would mean a new mistal. I can't afford it yet." He slowed his pace a little as they came near the entrance to the Stavethorpe Hall drive. "I'm leaving you here. I wish I knew what to say to Cyril, or to Bess, either."

"You'll think of something," Jenny assured him. Antony thought, with affection, that from anyone else he would have suspected a certain dryness in the remark, for Bill wasn't one to be tongue-tied; but Jenny meant just what she said. If things were different, if he could accept her loyalty easily, as she gave it, without this feeling of guilt. . . .

"I ought to be working," he told her when Bill had left them and they were getting over the stile. It occurred to him suddenly that what he had come out for was to retrace his last night's steps in daylight. Well, it wasn't a bad idea.

"You can't work all the time," said Jenny. She was wearing a camel coat so old as to be almost threadbare in places, and under it a "utility" suit—a horrible imitation of tweed in a shade of indeterminate green—that wasn't worth the coupons she had given for it, but she couldn't find anything else. But her walking shoes, also old, were neat and well polished, and her red cap and scarf achieved a cheerful air. She was swinging down the field beside him, trying to match his longer stride, and when she turned her head he saw that her gray eyes were sparkling. "It's a *beautiful* day," she said. "It makes me feel...I don't know...it's almost like being drunk.''

"Bless you, love; if drinking makes you look like that I wish we could afford it," Antony told her. Jenny put her head on one side, considering the remark.

"That's what Mrs. Dibb calls me," she said. "Luv," she added, by way of explanation.

"Do you mind?"

"No, I like it. Do you know what she said to me yesterday?"

"What?"

"'Let 'im do work, and thee look after t'brass.'"

"If that's her philosophy, she can't think much of me."

"No, she respects you. All that reading. Antony, what did Uncle Nick say when you told him we weren't coming home just yet?"

The phone call had been made two days before, but somehow they hadn't got around to talking about it. "He said no doubt I could waste my time here just as well as in London," said Antony, carefully exact.

And wasn't surprised when Jenny gave a relieved sigh and said, "That's all right, then," because coming from Sir Nicholas Harding that was the equivalent of an enthusiastic endorsement of their intention.

"He also said the plumbers were going in this week. We're as well out of the way."

"Poor Uncle Nick, he does hate the upset."

"He'll get over it. Anyway, it was his idea."

"Yes, I know. Antony, you do like the arrangement, don't you?"

"A place of our own? Of course I do."

"I just wondered—"

She let the sentence trail off into silence, and as Antony didn't seem to have anything else to say they walked on without speaking for a while. Past the Claytons' cottage, which faced west up the valley—a modest holding, its four acres enclosed by walls that were exceptionally well maintained. "Bill says Grandpa Clayton was the champion dry-stone waller for miles around," said Jenny, but Antony hadn't anything to say to that, either.

The crossing at Riddingstones was simple enough by daylight, and at the other side the path upstream was well marked. There was a cottage called Deansthorpe a little way up the hill, whose sole occupant was an old man called Cunliffe...unless you could count a couple of hogs and a scatter of Rhode Island Reds in the yard as company. Come to think of it, there hadn't been a light there last night; perhaps the old boy went to bed when darkness fell. He must be something of an eccentric, as he was reputed to use old sacks as curtains, changing his brand of feed when he felt in need of a change of color. The cottage was too far from the path to see if this was true. Of course everybody in Thorburndale used sacks over their heads as a protection in wet weather, looking in consequence very much like illustrations from the Luttrell Psalter, so perhaps their use as curtain material wasn't so very odd after all.

They had come by now into the shadow of the wood that surrounded Dallow Park. Last night the trees had looked ghostlike in the moonlight, but he had been glad enough of the shelter they afforded. Today the sun filtered through leafless branches, and the waters of the Thorburn, burbling happily along its stony bed, were sunlit, too. From here you couldn't see the house, though from Brass Castle it was clearly visible, rising rather gauntly above the line of trees. They were nearing the bridge, and Jenny was saying, "I don't think I believe in witches," when a man on horseback came out of one of the rides, a few paces ahead of them. He reined to a halt when he saw them coming, and waited for them to come alongside.

The horse was a fine chestnut, and its rider was, in his own way, equally good-looking—a heavily built man, perhaps in his fifties, with gray hair growing in rather tight waves over a well-shaped head, and an impressive nose and chin. He raised a hand in greeting, and said in a friendly voice, "You must be Cleveland's visitors at Brass Castle."

Antony said, "Yes, we are." Jenny contented herself with smiling, and came up closer, so that she could rub the chestnut's nose. He seemed to appreciate the attention, and bent his head to see if there was any sugar in her pockets.

The horseman said, "I'm Wilfred Damerel. I have heard your names, but I'm afraid I don't—"

"Antony Maitland, sir. This is my wife, Jenny." He paused a moment, until the usual polite murmuring that follows an introduction had subsided. "If I remember what Bill told me correctly, you own Dallow Park."

"I do."

"I hope we're not trespassing."

"It wouldn't matter, but as a matter of fact there's a right of way all along this side of the river, and up through the woods, too."

Jenny, who had been turning her pockets out to convince her new friend of their emptiness, looked up and smiled. "It's beautiful country."

"It is, indeed." He smiled in his turn. "Local gossip has you as a couple of Londoners, but I must say you look very much at home."

"We live in London now, but we both came from Sussex originally."

"That explains it, then. Are you interested in old houses? You must come and see the Park; it has the distinction of being one of the most uncomfortable houses in Yorkshire.''

"It looks . . . rather grim,'' said Antony cautiously.

"Doesn't it? It was one of the royal hunting lodges, originally . . . all this land was part of the Forest of Knaresborough, you know. We held it for the king until the Restoration, when Charles II gave it to us outright . . . in consideration, I suppose, for favors received. What favors, it is probably best not to inquire.''

"It's a long time ago.''

"So it is. Well, I mustn't keep you standing. I'm just going over to Stavethorpe Hall. Cleveland has heard, I suppose, about Hester Thornton's death.''

"Mrs. Dibb told us last night.''

"Ah, yes, Mrs. Dibb.''

"Bill's there now, as a matter of fact. At Stavethorpe Hall, I mean.''

"I shall see him, then. Goodbye, Mrs. Maitland. I'll get my daughter to telephone you, perhaps on the weekend. That's something else I heard on the local grapevine . . . that Cleveland managed to persuade the powers-that-be to give him a telephone.''

"He told them he'd hold them personally responsible if his sows were ill and he couldn't get the vet in time.''

"And it worked?''

"The phone's there to prove it.''

"We shall call you, then.''

Jenny stood watching him as he rode away, until a bend in the path hid him from sight. "What a nice man.''

"You're as bad as Bill. Nice, indeed!''

"Well, friendly, then. Pleasant. Don't you like him, Antony?''

"Yes, very much.'' He began to walk on toward the bridge. "I was only complaining about your choice of words.''

"There aren't so many to choose from," said Jenny, following him.

"The English language is the richest—"

"Yes, I daresay. Don't let's go straight back, Antony. I want to see where the witches used to meet in How Gill."

"Just as you like." It was what he had intended all along, but now some spirit of contrariness made him argue. "You said just now you didn't believe—"

"Not in the daytime."

"Anyway, you've been through How Gill before."

"But we weren't looking for anything then."

He relented and smiled at her. "All right, we'll make a pilgrimage. You do realize, don't you, that there'll most likely be nothing to see?"

How Gill was about half a mile upstream from the packhorse bridge, which was the most direct route back to Brass Castle, and the dictionary definition of a gill (a deep, usually wooded, ravine) fitted it to perfection. Both banks sloped steeply, with the water tumbling between to join the Thorburn, but there was sufficient flat ground at the river's edge to leave the footpath easy walking, and the plank bridge, with its rustic handrail, looked safe enough. Halfway up the bank on the other side was a stone building, a barn of some sort, that Antony couldn't remember having noticed before, but it wasn't until they had crossed the bridge and, leaving the path, climbed a little way among the trees that they saw the clearing. It was roughly circular, about fifty feet across, carpeted with dead leaves, and the trees growing densely around it, except where the corner of the barn projected. Jenny stood at the edge and looked around her, and said in a tone that betrayed her disappointment, "It's creepy, isn't it? It looks as if nobody had been here since the beginning of time. But there's nothing to show—"

"Wait a bit." Antony was crossing the clearing,

and the leaves rustled underfoot as he went. The sounds he had heard the previous night might well have come from here, but he hadn't any conscious hope of finding any sign either of Norman's witches or of any other intruder. Even so, it was with a feeling of inevitability that he saw the cigarette, barely a quarter smoked, that had been stamped out close against the barn wall. "Someone's been here." He sounded amused. "Do you suppose . . . do witches smoke Player's?"

Jenny came across to join him. "What a sell! Anybody may have dropped it."

"Very true. Anybody, at any time," said Antony thoughtfully. "But fancy wasting good tobacco, when it's still so scarce." He caught Jenny's eye, and added for her benefit, "It doesn't prove anything, either way. What were you expecting to see?"

"I don't know. Some signs of revelry by night, I suppose."

"Do you really believe—?"

"Not really. I thought *you* expected to find something," she said, with more shrewdness than he had bargained for. And then, when he made no immediate reply, "Is there a house near here?"

"Burntside Hall. Somewhere up there, I imagine." He gestured vaguely up the hill. "The manager of one of the banks in Great Allerton lives there, so Bill says. Now, there's a thought! Perhaps he runs the coven."

Jenny laughed at that. "Beautifully inappropriate," she said with appreciation. "There'd have to be twelve people, wouldn't there?"

"Thirteen altogether."

"Well, anyway, I can't imagine where they'd come from." She stirred the thick mat of leaves with her toe. "But if the whole neighborhood came together and danced from dusk to dawn, there wouldn't be any sign of it. Do you suppose Norman really believes—?"

"I don't know. He said something else, Jenny. He said there was a rumor that Mrs. Thornton's death was caused by witchcraft, but I promised not to tell Bill about that."

"So that's what Mrs. Dibb meant when she said there was talk."

"Yes, but it might mean, mightn't it, that the country people are uneasy about her death? Do you suppose Thornton murdered her?"

"Bill likes him," Jenny objected.

"He also said Mrs. Thornton was a termagant. And they *are* having an autopsy," Antony reminded her.

"You said yourself that was just a formality."

"I know I did. All the same it's interesting... don't you think?"

"I don't believe a word of it."

"It's a far cry from the witches, certainly, but more likely on the whole." He glanced at his watch, and held out his hand to her. "There isn't time to go around by Winterscale. Shall we be going back?"

## 3

THEY FOUND BILL already changed into his working clothes, but glad enough to break off what he was doing when he saw them coming up the field. "How did you find things at Stavethorpe?" asked Jenny as he joined them.

"As you'd expect." Bill wasn't one to show his feelings, but they both thought he was troubled. "Hester's death was bad enough, of course, but now there's this question—Doctor Todd wouldn't sign the certificate."

"Why not?"

"Because he didn't expect... she'd been having these bilious attacks on and off for several months now. Worrying, but not fatal... that's what he thought. Then the last one was unexpectedly severe."

"I see."

"Cyril thinks he must have overlooked something. It'll all be cleared up by the post mortem, but of course he hates the idea of *that*. So does Bess. The inquest's on Friday."

"How is Bess today?" asked Jenny. "Mrs. Dibb said she was tired out."

"So she is, but she isn't one to complain. Hester was taken ill on Saturday evening. The doctor came, of course, but there was no getting a nurse, and at that time he wasn't too perturbed about her condition. It was only when he saw her yesterday that he became really worried.

Cyril and Bess had been up with her all night."

"What were the symptoms?"

"I don't know, except that she was violently sick, and restless in between the fits of sickness. Does that tell you anything?"

"Not a thing."

"Could it have been food poisoning?" Jenny suggested.

"It sounds like that, doesn't it? But she hadn't had anything to eat that the others hadn't had, too, or so Cyril said. Anyway, it's not so usual in midwinter, I shouldn't think."

"Was it your friend Sergeant Newbould whose car I saw?"

"Yes, but he only stayed ten minutes. Said it'd be time enough to worry them if the results of the post mortem...well, if she'd been poisoned, I suppose he meant."

"Is that what the doctor had in mind?"

"I should think it must have been, wouldn't you? But I don't see how it could have happened...I mean, any more than food poisoning. The others would have got it, too."

There wasn't anything to be gained by pointing out the obvious alternatives to accidental death. They must have occurred to Bill already, but it wasn't to be expected that he'd say so. Antony said, "Yes, I see what you mean," and was glad when he heard Mrs. Dibb calling them in to dinner. They went up through the kitchen garden and into the house.

Dinner was roast pork...fresh pork, for a change. "We always have it when one of our neighbors kills," said Bill. "And in due course we return the compliment. All strictly illegal, of course." If he was worried about the state of affairs at Stavethorpe Hall, he seemed to have put it momentarily behind him.

"We met another of your neighbors, a chap called Damerel," said Antony, passing his plate to Jenny for more potatoes. "Did you see him?"

"Yes, he arrived just as I was leaving. Which reminds me, I phoned Arthur Micklefield when I got back. He asked you and Jenny for tea this afternoon."

"I ought—"

"One afternoon won't make any difference. You can read all the evening, for that matter, if you really want to."

"The trouble is," said Antony with unusual frankness, "I don't."

Bill looked as if he might be going to comment on that, but stopped himself at the last moment. Jenny said, "It's the big house on the left, isn't it, just after you pass Ferrens Point?"

"That's right. All you can actually see from the road is the roof and chimneys. It's built into the side of the hill, as we are, but nearer the road. The farm buildings are on the other side—if you ever take the car along there, Jenny, you'll have to be careful not to run over any of Arthur's hens—but the land runs down the hill, a narrowish strip, right to the river's edge."

"What time should we go?"

"It'll take you about twenty minutes. If you leave here at half-past three . . . that will give you nearly two hours for your books, Antony, if your conscience is really troubling you. And Jenny can help me put up the evening feed."

II

ARTHUR MICKLEFIELD AND HIS WIFE, EMILY, were elderly, and—as sometimes happens with long-married couples—might easily have been taken for brother and sister. Both were tallish and thin, with

straight gray hair and rather faded blue eyes. The
only real difference was that he stooped a little,
while she stood very erect. Their house, Ferrenscross, was old...perhaps even older than Brass
Castle, which dated from about the year 1600; but
the layout was far more complicated. It had obviously always been a gentleman's residence. "You
will see," said Professor Micklefield, greeting the
Maitlands on the doorstep with every appearance of
pleasure, "that we bear the honorable scars of violence during the Civil War." The front door, of
stout oak planks studded with large-headed iron
nails, certainly looked rather battered. Inside were
the familiar flagged floor, an oak table well polished and dark with age, and a rug with a delicate
and inappropriate pattern, which looked to Antony
as if it might be valuable.

The room on the left of the hall to which they
were led was large and dim, with a lattice window
and a roaring log fire. Jenny said, "How lovely!"
and stretched her hands to the blaze.

Mrs. Micklefield smiled at her and said in her gentle way, "We think it best not to inquire too closely
where Seth gets the wood. We should certainly be
in difficulties without it."

"I don't really know that we're contravening any
regulation," the professor added, "but it's difficult
to do anything at all these days without breaking
the law."

They were all seated by this time. "Bill says the
worst thing is petrol rationing," said Jenny. "He
has enough to get to market once a week, but not
for visiting friends."

"Being cold would be worse."

"Or not having enough hot water."

"Or if we didn't have our own eggs and milk and
bacon. I don't know how people manage in town at
all."

Perhaps it was as well that the tea was brought in just then, or the exchange of grievances might have gone on indefinitely. It was brought by a youngish dumpling of a woman in a flowered overall that was limp from many washings, and certainly the array of scones and cake and sandwiches did nothing to remind them of the current shortage of food. "Everything's homemade," said Mrs. Micklefield, looking from Jenny to Antony and thinking, perhaps, that they could both do with feeding up. "Daisy really is a treasure."

"Bill tells me you're interested in the local history," said the professor, when the tea had been poured and they had all settled down again. "This house, for instance, was owned in the seventeenth century by some people called Plumpton, a branch of the Pickering family. They were royalist; so presumably the marks on the door were made by the parliamentary forces, but I have never been able to discover exactly what happened."

"They'd have burned the place, wouldn't they, if they'd got in?"

"Very probably. My own theory is that they were an unofficial party of marauders, that they were interrupted in some way, or called off to take part in some more important engagement."

"I hadn't thought of Thorburndale in connection with the Civil War."

"Oh, yes, indeed. Surely Bill has told you that two cannons were detached from the siege of York and brought to Ferrens Point to bombard Dallow Park."

"Good Lord!"

"Old Noll himself—Cromwell, of course—is said to have been present, but that part of the story I take leave to doubt."

"But why should they bother to do that?"

"It was a royal hunting lodge."

"We met Mr. Damerel this morning. He told us that."

"It is difficult, as a matter of fact, to adduce any motive for what was done other than spite. Two sons of the family were with the royalist forces. . . d'Aumerle they were in those days. The rest of the story—also, I think, apocryphal—is that Prince Rupert himself raised the siege. . . if it can be dignified by that name. Otherwise the house would have been destroyed."

"I don't think Bill knows all this."

"He'd have been bound to tell us," said Jenny.

"He has, after all, been busy since he came to these parts." Micklefield picked up Jenny's cup and passed it to his wife. "Tell me, how are things going with him?"

It ought to have been the most casual question, no more meaningful than "how d'you do?" For some reason it struck Antony that there was more to it than that, that the answer was awaited almost with anxiety. He said, "Very well, so far as I can tell," in rather a reserved tone.

But Jenny, who had obviously seen nothing odd in the professor's manner, added eagerly, "The farm is marvelous. He bought some of his stock from you, didn't he?"

"A couple of gilts in pig. The first one, I know, didn't turn out too well."

Jenny laughed. "That's the one Bill calls 'the wicked Lady Pig.' She's bacon now. . . *lean* bacon. Nothing would make her fat, he said, and she had the most contrary nature."

"Her litter was the important thing."

"She only reared four. But the other one—Grunter—is wonderful."

"Ferrenscross Snowflake," murmured Antony, whom the name had struck as humorous.

"Yes. . . well, she's got her second litter now, and

she's never laid on one. And she'll do anything you want, as long as you can make her understand what it is... which isn't always so easy.''

Professor Micklefield smiled at her. "You ought to talk to Seth Dodgson, my dear. He's another enthusiast.''

"Is he? I never realized before that pigs all have different personalities. Grunter worries, for instance... you can see her doing it. But, of course, you know much more about them than I do.''

"I'm afraid I'm the merest amateur.'' He glanced at Antony, who had been listening to this exchange with some amusement and—abetted by Mrs. Micklefield—concentrating on his tea. "But as long as things are going well at Brass Castle—''

Again it was Jenny who answered him, saying cheerfully, "Oh, they are! And Bill's so happy there.''

"Is he going to expand his milking herd, do you know?''

"I don't think so.''

"That's Norman's idea,'' Antony put in. "But what we really wanted to ask you, sir, was to tell us about the local history of witchcraft.''

"Why was that, I wonder.''

"Because we heard a rumor—from Norman Dibb, of all people—that there's a coven operating in these parts again.''

"I should think it very unlikely.''

"So should I, but it made me wonder—''

The professor exchanged a look with his wife, and seemed to make up his mind. "There is a story going about,'' he confirmed. "I can see it might make you curious—'' He broke off, got up, and crossed the room to an old-fashioned secretary with a bookcase above. "The best book dealing with the subject in these parts is undoubtedly Fairfax's *Daemon-ologia*,'' he said, as he pulled open the door. "Here

we are: *A discourse on witchcraft as it was acted in
the family of Mr. Edward Fairfax of Fuystone in
the county of York in the year A.D. 1621.*'' He came
back to the group by the fire, holding the book between his hands; it was an old book in a mottled
brown binding, and he handled it lovingly.

"Fewston is in Washburndale, isn't it?"

"That's right. Not so very many miles from here,
as the crow flies, though it's a fair way around by
road. Fairfax says of himself that he is 'neither fantastic Puritan or superstitious Papist,' but for all
that he must have been a bit of an eccentric. He
came to write his book because eight women whom
he had accused of witchcraft—in fact, of obtaining
the death of one of his daughters by their 'arts and
spells'—were tried at York and acquitted; so he had,
I suppose, to get rid of his spleen in some other
way."

"He must have believed it all."

"I'm sure he did." He was turning the pages as he
spoke. "But he didn't reserve his strictures for the
eight who were tried, you know. There's this:
'many suspected of witchcraft lived in the forest in
Fuystone parish—people suffered great losses, particularly kine—went to wise men or wizards, and
burnt young calves alive and the like—' "

"How horrible," said Jenny, shuddering. He gave
her a smile, but went on without interruption.

" '—whereof I know that experiments have been
made by the best sort of my neighbors, and thereby
they have found help as they report. So little is the
truth of the Christian religion known in this wild
place, and rude people, upon whose ignorance God
have mercy.' "

"If anybody tried that kind of thing today there'd
be no keeping it dark."

"No, indeed." He closed the book and restored it
carefully to its place on the shelf before going back

to his chair again. "But I was telling you: Fairfax
had a neighbor, Henry Robinson, whose first wife,
Anne, was said to have been bewitched to death by
the witches of Lancashire. His second wife, Jennet,
had suicidal and homicidal tendencies. . .the latter
directed, apparently, against her own children.
Now I have read somewhere that between the two
men there was 'some unkindness and question of
law'—I think I am quoting correctly—so perhaps we
should not place too much emphasis on what Edward Fairfax has to say on this matter."

"What does he say, sir?"

"Concerning Henry Robinson, that one of the
eight witches was 'very familiar in his house.' That
is as far as the written evidence goes. But in Thorburndale it is held that the woman concerned came
from hereabouts, that she was young and very
beautiful, and that it was because she used her
wiles on the judge that the eight were acquitted."

"That lends a certain éclat to the story, doesn't
it?"

"Oh, I agree. The trouble is—" again he seemed to
take counsel with his wife "—that it lies at the root
of the rumor that you have heard today."

"I don't quite understand."

"I was told it by Fay Dodgson, who is, I'm afraid,
inclined to gossip, and I should not be repeating it if
you had not already heard—"

He broke off, and Jenny said into the silence that
followed, "Mrs. Dibb said it was wicked talk."

"That describes it exactly, but it is better, perhaps,
that you should hear it from me. You see, the story
that is going around not only concerns the revival of
the local coven—that would be comparatively harmless—but refers to one particular person. A girl who
is said to be the descendant—a reincarnation, perhaps—of the witch who was on familiar terms with
Henry Robinson."

"But why—?"

"I'm afraid coincidence has been at work. The name is the same in both cases, which seems to be regarded as evidence enough."

"Somebody living locally?"

"Bess Foster."

Jenny said incredulously, "But they can't really believe—"

"The idea has been given a certain amount of credence by the country people, I'm sorry to say."

"But—" Antony was as taken aback as Jenny was, and he spoke slowly, trying to think it out. "That explains what Norman said to me: that 'they' were saying Mrs. Thornton died by witchcraft."

"Yes."

"Nobody could possibly believe—"

"You don't know how an idea can stay alive in a country district. . .through the years, through the centuries even."

"What exactly is being said?"

"In round terms, that Bess Foster is Thornton's mistress, and that Hester Thornton died because she was bewitched."

"Is that why the doctor. . .oh, no, surely he can't believe it, too?"

Micklefield laughed at that. "Todd? No, I don't think so. It is unfortunate, however, that this question has arisen, because it has certainly given the gossips something to get their teeth into."

"I should say it had." Antony got up to hand his cup to Mrs. Micklefield, but when it had been refilled he went to stand with his back to the fire, instead of resuming his seat. "The inquest is on Friday," he said with an inquiring note in his voice.

"Unfortunately, whatever verdict is brought in it is unlikely that the rumor will be silenced."

"No, I see that. It's an awkward situation, isn't it?"

"I needn't ask you—"

"We shan't talk about it . . . naturally. Only if Bill hears half the story, I shall tell him."

"Yes, of course. We must hope that won't happen." He turned to Jenny and smiled at her. "You'll be thinking you've come to a strange part of the world, my dear."

She shook her head. "Not really. I wanted to hear about the witches, you know, but I'd no idea the real story would be so nasty."

"Then I advise you to forget it. At least, it is unlikely to do anyone any harm."

"It would worry Bess Foster . . . it would be bound to worry her if she heard about it."

"Nobody is going to repeat it to her, or to Cyril Thornton."

"I should hope not." Jenny sounded shocked.

Antony shifted his position a little, out of the direct range of the fire, and said soberly, "Part of the story, at least, would be of interest to the police if they find that Mrs. Thornton was poisoned."

"But that is surely of all things the most unlikely," the professor protested.

"I don't know enough of the circumstances to hazard a guess." He shrugged, and drank what was left of his tea, and leaned forward to put the cup down on the tray.

"I assure you, one part of the story is as . . . as unbelievable as the rest."

The professor sounded troubled now, and Jenny said, answering the tone rather than the words, "You can't help what the country people say."

"No . . . of course. But, in a way, it might have been worse."

"How do you mean?"

"If they had fixed upon Cyril as the culprit. It is an open secret that Hester was the one with money—the police might have found that a more convincing motive. But enough of that. Let me think what I can tell you of a more cheerful nature," he said, smiling at Jenny. "We were speaking of Dallow Park and the Damerel family. Something tells me that your friend Bill has not heard the legend that connects them with Brass Castle."

"If he has, he hasn't mentioned it."

"I'm sure he would have been bound to do so. It is strange, really, that I have never thought to mention it to him, but we have always talked of farming matters, not of history. Not that this is history, of course; another tale that has been passed down by word of mouth."

"Bill was quite right to tell us to come to you."

"Yes, this story I think you will enjoy. By some means, it is said, the Damerels got wind of the proposed attack on Dallow Park, and all their treasure was given into the keeping of a servant, who hid it at Brass Castle."

"That explains the name, then," said Antony. "I always thought it was an odd one for what must originally have been quite a small holding."

"Yes, but... would they have much 'treasure'?" asked Jenny doubtfully.

"So the story goes. They are an old family, you know. Their own gold and jewels, and the church plate from Saint Wilfred's at Priest Monkton, which had been entrusted to them for safekeeping in those troubled times."

"Where was it hidden, do you know?"

"Nobody knows that. I haven't made myself clear, I'm afraid. The treasure has been missing from that day to this."

"But why... why on earth didn't they dig it up again when the crisis was over?" Jenny sounded almost indignant.

"That wasn't for some time. All this happened

two days before Marston Moor was fought, and
after that parliament's star was in the ascendant,
here in the north as well as in other parts of the
country. I expect it was thought more prudent to
leave things as they were. The Damerels kept their
land, for which, I imagine, they can thank the
remote district in which we live. But one of the sons
was in exile until the Restoration. By that time,
who knows what may have happened?''

While the professor was speaking, Antony had
gone back to his chair again. He said now, ''Was the
servant honest?''

''A trusted servant, certainly.''

''That's the easiest explanation, isn't it? That
they looked for the treasure and it wasn't there.''

''I can only tell you the legend...that it has
never been recovered.''

''Hasn't anyone ever looked for it?''

''Indeed they have. There was an expedition of
students from Leeds University here one summer,
not long before the war.''

''Under your guidance, sir?''

''With my enthusiastic help. Unfortunately I
knew no more than the rest of them where to
look.''

''So what did you do?''

''We dug up the whole of the kitchen garden, for
one thing, and a very laborious job it was. We even
went so far as to take up the floor in one of the
buildings. Then we explored as well as we could
around anything that could be regarded as a land-
mark...the spring in the top field, the various gate-
ways. We didn't have to cover the whole of the
present farmlands, you know; the original holding
was not more than twenty acres. And we had a
diviner in...they're said to be able to find metals
as well as water. But all to no avail.''

''Didn't the owner mind?''

"Seth Dodgson was living there at the time, my present bailiff. He bore with us very well."

"You must have been awfully disappointed," said Jenny with sympathy. "But surely the Damerels looked... after the Restoration, when they were safe again."

"Wilfred says they did, but with no better luck than the rest of us."

"Isn't there anything... any written history?"

"There's a book by a man called Clough, written in the latter part of the nineteenth century, that gives the place that the treasure was hidden as Burntside Hall; but in spite of this the local version of the story is very strongly in favor of Brass Castle."

"Burntside Hall," repeated Antony slowly.

"Yes, but as I say—" He seemed to decide he had said enough, and let the sentence trail into silence. "The only other source of information is the parish records... Saint John's in Winterscale, that is. They tell us that a family called Ambler lived at Brass Castle at that time. Richard Ambler married Margaret Noble in 1615, and they had three children; Hugh, and Helen, and another, Margaret. I forget the actual dates of their birth. Margaret married one Simon Thorpe in August, 1644, and died in 1686. Helen died in 1650, apparently unmarried. There is no record of what happened to Hugh. Which of them was the servant who disposed of the treasure is anybody's guess."

"Hugh, perhaps," Antony suggested. "He made his fortune, and went away to live riotously on the proceeds."

Micklefield smiled. "As to that, I doubt if anybody could live riotously during the Commonwealth."

"Then he went abroad. I'd rather think that someone had some fun out of it, than that it's still moldering in the ground."

"Even a thief?"

"Well, no, perhaps not. What do you think of the story, sir? Is it true?"

"If I had to guess I should say that the part about the missing treasure is founded on fact. Whether it was ever at Brass Castle is another matter."

"So it's no use hoping that one of the pigs will root it up one day."

"Not a bit of use, I'm afraid. But I've done enough talking for one afternoon. Tell us something about yourselves."

"There's nothing to tell," said Jenny, not very originally. She carefully did not look at her husband as she spoke; it was the sort of open invitation that raised his hackles at once, leading as it inevitably did to a question about his wartime activities. "Antony's reading law, and I'm just a housewife...or shall be when we get a home of our own."

"That's not always so easy these days."

"No, but we're lucky. Antony's uncle is letting us have the two top floors of his house. The plumbers are in now, so with any luck there'll be nothing to do when we get home except the decorating. We've even got some furniture...some from Uncle Nick, and some from my home, so you see—"

She broke off there, and Mrs. Micklefield said placidly, "How nice for you." And then, looking from one of them to the other, "How long have you been married?"

"Four years this month."

"Good heavens!" said the professor. "I'm sorry, my dear, that was rude of me, but you don't look old enough—"

"I'm twenty-two," said Jenny, a little on her dignity, but not much because their curiosity was so very friendly.

"A war wedding," said Mrs. Micklefield, and let her eyes rest on Antony for a moment in a considering way, so that at once he was on the defensive, thinking she had noticed that he held himself a little stiffly, or perhaps—even worse—that he had only the limited use of his right arm. "You were in one of the services, I suppose. Which one?"

"The army." As little as Jenny did he want to snub them, but the words came abruptly and he couldn't think of anything to add to them, so that there was a silence, long enough for discomfort.

Jenny thought, anyone would think he'd done something to be ashamed of, but it wasn't in her nature to be critical, even if she hadn't understood his motives fairly well, that he couldn't bear to be reminded. So she said lightly, "It seems a long time ago. It's a year now since Antony was demobilized," and both the Micklefields turned to her with something like gratitude, and began again to discuss the perennial topic of peacetime shortages, which was more than enough to keep them busy until it was time for Antony and Jenny to leave. Antony had recovered his poise by that time, and expressed his gratitude becomingly, both for the tea and the history lesson.

# 4

IT WAS NEARLY DARK OUTSIDE, but not quite dark enough for them to need the flashlight Jenny had brought with her. They climbed the hill in silence until they came again to High Lane, with Ferrens Point on their right. Then Antony said explosively, as though the question had been bottled up for a long time, "Why the devil do you suppose he told us that story?"

Jenny didn't attempt to misunderstand him. "You mean, about Bess Foster."

"Yes, of course."

"I think it was because . . . I've got a nasty feeling he half believes it himself."

"He couldn't."

"Why not?"

"He's too intelligent." ("You're an educated man," Norman had said. If that was true—or even if it wasn't—it applied far more strongly to the professor. But was that any guarantee he wouldn't, at the same time, be superstitious?)

"Why do *you* think he told us, then?"

"Because he knows, or guesses, that Bill is interested in the girl."

"Even so—"

"It's fair enough . . . if he decided he could trust our discretion. Then we can tell Bill if it seems advisable for him to know. Not otherwise."

"I'd hate to have to tell him. I mean, the witch business is just nonsense, but the rest of it—"

"The rumor that she's Thornton's mistress," said Antony, taking the idea out and looking at it. "If Sergeant Newbould had heard that he might have spent more than ten minutes at Stavethorpe Hall the other night."

"And I did so hope that Bill—"

"Jenny, love, we don't *know* anything."

"No, I suppose not."

"There's another thing. . . is Bill worried?"

"He was worried last night about Bess, and perhaps about Mr. Thornton, too."

"I didn't mean that. . . about the farm. About the way things are going."

"I don't think so."

"Neither do I. It was the way old Micklefield asked us that made me curious, as if he had some inside information. Never mind, I expect I'm imagining things."

When they came to the gate there was a bicycle leaning against the wall—a sturdy machine, but one that looked as if it had seen better days. Antony said, "A visitor," but before he could get the gate open a tall figure had loomed up out of the dusk. A police constable looking, for no very obvious reason, an unlikely figure in those wild surroundings.

"Good evening. You'll be Mr. and Mrs. Maitland, I wouldn't wonder," he said as he came up to them.

"That's right." They ought to be used by now to being recognized as the only strangers in the district, but for all that Antony sounded a little surprised.

"Constable Lister." It was impossible to see his face clearly, but his voice had the local accent, though it was broader and softer than Norman Dibb's. "Mr. Cleveland said I might meet you."

"Can we help you?"

"Well, now, I don't know that." He wasn't going to be hurried. "It's about t'black market."

Jenny started to say something, but Antony's hand on her arm silenced her. He said, "I don't see how we can. *Is* there a black market in Thorburn-dale?"

The constable ignored this, except to say ponderously, "Acting on information received."

"I see," said Antony blankly.

"They tell me you're a walker, Mr. Maitland. All hours of the day and night. . .that's what they say."

"That isn't quite accurate, but I do sometimes go out in the evening." There was an edge to his voice that Jenny noticed, though the constable seemed unaware of it.

"Well, now," said Constable Lister, who seemed to be addicted to the phrase, "did you ever see anything. . .anything suspicious like?"

"Why. . .no. I'm not at all sure I know what kind of thing you mean. Can you tell me?"

"I can an' all. Anybody loading up a truck at night, say. Or any other time, for that matter, except on market day."

"That's more difficult. I see a certain amount of traffic, of course, and that includes an occasional cattle truck, but I keep to the footpaths as much as possible, not to the roads."

"Nothing suspicious, then?"

"No."

"Or anything that might lead you to think there was some illegal slaughtering going on."

"I'm afraid I haven't seen or heard anything that could help you." His mind had gone back to How Gill, of course, but still the statement was strictly true.

Constable Lister heaved a sigh. "It'd be too much to expect," he said sadly, "to have t'evidence handed to us on a plate. I'll be saying good-night to you, and thank you. I'd best be getting on my way."

He pushed his bicycle out into the road, swung into the saddle and pedaled away, his cape billowing in the evening breeze, so that in the twilight he looked like nothing so much as a great bat.

They both stood looking after him for a moment before setting off down the Iron Age track. It was darker here, between the high walls of earth, and after Jenny had stumbled a couple of times she gave in and used the flashlight. So they came to the Brass Castle gate, with the twisted larch tree beside it leaning away from the prevailing southwest wind in perpetual and futile flight.

Jenny said, "Brrr . . . I shall be glad to get inside."

And Antony said, "Yes, it is cold again," carefully not agreeing with her. She thought he was still thinking of Constable Lister, and the questions to which, these days, he never seemed to be able to reconcile himself, but his mind had gone back to what Professor Micklefield had told them, and he couldn't help feeling it might create an awkwardness. . . .

Bill was writing up his milk records when they went in, but he closed the book firmly when he saw them, moved the oil lamp from the table to the sideboard, and went over to the fire. "Shut the door, Antony," he commanded. "It's cold."

"I'm sorry." He hadn't realized he had left it standing open to the night air, but now he turned and closed it carefully, as though it was a difficult task that required all his concentration.

"Did you meet Constable Lister, by any chance?" Bill asked, as they shed their coats and joined him.

"We did," said Antony, adding in a hollow tone, "Be sure your sins will find you out."

"I thought they had, for an awful moment."

"Don't be silly," said Jenny crossly. "You know you wouldn't—"

"The phrase 'black market' can cover a multitude

of sins," Bill told her, "from organized crime to
changing a pound of sugar for a packet of tea.
Ninety-nine percent of the population must be
guilty in some way or another."

"Well, yes, perhaps, but not things the police are
interested in," she protested.

Antony, toasting himself luxuriously in front of
the fire, was rather pleased with the turn the conversation had taken, away from the Thorntons' affairs. "What's your particular sin, Bill?" he asked
lightly.

"Selling bacon to the clergy. And ham, of
course."

"How appalling."

"You see, the parish priest in Great Allerton—the
Catholic priest, that is—had a new curate straight
from Ireland who didn't have any idea about rationing, of course, and who was eating him out of house
and home. So, as we can kill two pigs a year for our
own use, and weren't here for the whole of 1946,
either. . . . You aren't supposed to sell any of it, but
I can't say I've lost any sleep over the deal."

"An act of charity, you might say. What did this
Constable Lister really want?"

"Didn't he tell you? There's been a lot of black-
market meat turning up in centers like Leeds and
Rothershaw. It could have come from this area,
although there are other possibilities. I think the
country police in general have been asked to have a
look around."

"So long as you keep your head—"

"It isn't all that funny, as a matter of fact. Lister
said it was pretty clear the whole thing is organized
on quite a large scale, and they're not above violence. . . . A butcher in Rothershaw was beaten up
quite badly, and is still on the danger list. Constable
Lister seemed to think it was all part of the same
thing."

"That explains the trend of his questions, then."
Jenny, alert to every change of tone, thought he had
quite got over his moodiness now. "The trouble is, I
wouldn't necessarily know a stranger if I saw one."

"*Have* you seen anything suspicious?"

"Not a thing."

"I don't suppose it has anything to do with
Thorburndale."

"Probably not. Does your friend the bank manager...?"

"Undercliffe."

"Yes. Does he do any farming?"

"Now what maggot have you got into your
head?"

"I was just wondering," said Antony vaguely.

"Well, he doesn't. Burntside Hall had some land
originally, I expect, but now there are just the
grounds—not more than a couple of acres in all."

"I see."

Bill didn't look altogether satisfied, but it was
obvious that Antony wasn't going to say anything
more, so he turned the subject obligingly. "It must
be galling for Lister to be investigating the black
market, when what he's always wanted is a good
murder mystery. He's the chap who, when told
there was a dead sheep on the river path at Winterscale, said it wasn't his job to do anything about it,
but added in a yearning tone, 'Now, if it had been a
*yewman* body—' I suppose it isn't really funny," he
added, recollecting himself when Antony and Jenny laughed, "when you think of Hester, I mean.
Let's talk of something more cheerful. How did you
get on with Professor Micklefield, for instance?"

"Very well. Lots of local color, and one thing that
will interest you, if you haven't already heard it...
a legend about Brass Castle."

"Nobody ever tells me anything," said Bill.
"What legend?"

"Just that the Damerels' treasure—it sounds dramatic, doesn't it—was hidden here by one of their servants during the Civil War, and has never been recovered."

"Do you mean we may be sitting on it?"

"It's quite possible. I should mention that the only book that refers to the subject says it was hidden at Burntside Hall, but the legend that it's here was strong enough to bring a party from Leeds University to investigate it."

"Without success, I trust."

"According to the professor, without any success at all."

"Then there's still hope," said Bill, amused. "Not that I fancy my chances of finding anything so unlikely as buried treasure and, anyway, it would still belong to the Damerels, I suppose."

"They might give you a cut if Grunter dug it up someday. Not that the professor thinks that's likely to happen. They covered all the likely spots pretty thoroughly, so he says."

"Well, that's an interesting sidelight, but not what you went to ask him, after all."

"He had a book about witchcraft as it was practiced in Washburndale in the early 1620s. I didn't ask him to lend it to me; it looked as if it might be valuable. And the local coven used to meet in How Gill, just as Norman said. I don't think he thought much of the idea that they were up to it again, though."

"I don't think much of it myself. Can you see Mrs. Dibb participating in an orgy, or whatever it was they used to get up to?"

"Not really." They seemed to have brushed past the possible difficulties quite well. Jenny was rather silent, but there was nothing unusual about that. Antony left his place on the hearth rug and settled down in the corner of the sofa nearest the fire. Their conversation continued in rather a desultory way. After a while Mrs. Dibb came in to lay the table for supper, but she had gone back to the kitchen and the three of them were alone again when there was a knock on the door. Bill got up to open it.

Antony, gazing into the fire, heard the slight, protesting squeak the door gave as it was pulled open, and felt the draft on the back of his neck. Bill said, "Bess!" in a startled tone, and then, "Come inside, you look frozen." Antony turned his head, and got his first look at Bess Foster, and was surprised into immobility for a moment before he recollected himself and came to his feet.

She was a tall girl with fair, straight hair, very soft and shining, that was drawn back into a bun that might have been old-fashioned, but certainly suited her. She was wearing a heavy tweed coat, with a blue woolen cap and scarf and gloves, but even now, with her face pale and rather pinched by the cold, there was no mistaking that she was a beauty. Later, when he made a catalog of her features, there didn't seem any special reason why this should be so. Her eyes were good—blue with dark brows and lashes—but there wasn't anything special to be said about her nose or mouth or chin, except that the total effect was stunning. If Bill had actually gone down for the count, thought Antony to himself, it wasn't surprising.

Bill was saying, "Jenny, this is Bess Foster. These are my friends, the Maitlands, Bess. . .Jenny and Antony. I've told you about them."

Bess smiled, but it was a mechanical gesture and went nowhere near her eyes. Then she looked at Bill and said urgently, "I'm sorry to arrive so unexpectedly, but I didn't know where else to go."

Jenny was on her feet by now. She went across the room to the newcomer, saying in a friendly tone, "Take your coat off, Bess, and come and sit by the fire. Then if you want to talk to Bill—"

"No!" said Bess. "I mean, don't go away." She smiled again, but it was still empty of any real meaning. "It's because you're here...it's really because you're here that I came."

This must have sounded like gibberish to Bill. Antony thought, here we go! He wasn't sure if Jenny had taken time to think the situation through, but whether she had or not she was dealing with it admirably. Under her coaxing Bess shed her outdoor things; she was wearing a dress of a soft shade of delphinium blue that made her eyes at once darker and more appealing. Jenny installed her in the seat by the fire that Antony had vacated, and said a little impatiently to Bill, who was standing by looking helpless, "Have we anything to drink?"

"Mrs. Dibb keeps some rum on hand for colds."

"Not rum. At least, I don't think—"

"No," said Bess.

"There's some of the sherry left that we had at New Year," Antony suggested. He was worried about what was coming, because he didn't want Bill to be hurt, but in spite of that he couldn't help taking a certain pleasure in the way Jenny was handling things. She was of so retiring a nature that he was always surprised, and a little touched, on the rare occasions when she took command. He was also extremely conscious of the picture the two girls made. As always, when the lamps were lighted, Jenny's hair shone more gold than brown, and she was wearing a garnet red dress that she had put on in honor of the Micklefields' tea party. For sheer looks, perhaps, she couldn't hold a candle to Bess, but there was something about her, a sort of serenity...someone it was worth coming home to, he thought irrelevantly, and did not realize at the time that the thought was in any way important.

"That'll do," said Jenny, accepting the offered sherry without enthusiasm. And Bill went to the sideboard for the bottle and a glass, which he over-filled, so that it had to be carried carefully to where Bess was sitting, and even more carefully taken from him and sipped. "That's better," said Jenny encouragingly. "You'll soon feel warmer." Bess looked up at her and smiled. She was undeniably, thought Antony, in the words Professor Micklefield had used, young and very beautiful. He went back to his favorite position with his back to the fire; Jenny sat down at the other end of the sofa, half turned toward Bess; and Bill took a chair at the opposite side of the hearth.

Antony thought, perhaps we should have warned him, but it was too late to worry about that now, and as nobody seemed to have anything to say and the silence was lengthening, he remarked tritely, "It's a cold night for a walk."

"It isn't that," said Bess quickly. "At least, it is cold, of course, but I didn't really notice."

"Something upset you," said Jenny.

"I suppose that's obvious. I didn't really mean to make a fuss." She drank some more of the sherry, and put the glass down on the table at her elbow. "It's what people are saying, you see. I don't really know what to do."

"What are they saying?" said Bill, in a grim tone that Antony had never heard from him before.

"That I—" She flushed scarlet and broke off, per-haps changing her mind about what she had been go-ing to say. "That I'm in love with Cyril and that—"

"What else?" asked Antony, prompting her when she came to a halt again.

"That . . . perhaps . . . that that's why Hester died," said Bess, completing the sentence in a rush.

Jenny put out a hand to cover hers comfortingly, but Bill came to his feet and said, still in that unfamiliar growl, "They're saying one of you killed her."

"I suppose . . . I think really . . . they mean me."

"But that's . . . that's libel," said Bill, as though the problem was a legal one.

Antony said, dragging them back to the point again, "Who told you that?" because the knowledge that she could sue someone for slander wasn't really going to help Bess at the moment.

She looked up at him helplessly and said in a hesitant way, "Mrs. Clayton. She said she thought I ought to know."

"Don't tell me she meant well," said Bill furiously. Antony thought it was time to get the conversation back onto a less heated plane. Bill didn't often lose his temper, in fact very rarely, indeed, but if he did he wouldn't be easy to handle.

"I'm a stranger here," he reminded them. "Who is Mrs. Clayton?" and was glad when Bill and Bess answered him in chorus, both of them sounding something nearer normal.

"She lives in the cottage near Riddingstones—"

"And comes to help in the house—"

"And her son helps on the farm. He's only about ninepence to the shilling—"

"But he's a good worker, Cyril says."

"I see. Now, from what you tell us, she did not herself accuse you."

"No, she was all righteous indignation." Bess had some color in her cheeks now, and he was glad to see a sparkle of anger in her eye. Anything was better than the state of shock she had arrived in. "She said she thought I ought to know what 'they' were saying."

"Mrs. Dibb told me about her," said Jenny. She glanced at Bill, as if she was trying to gauge the effect of her words on him. "She says Mrs. Clayton's a foreigner—I think that only means she comes from

Leeds—and doesn't like Thorburndale or any of her neighbors.''

''Why does she stay here, then?''

''That's what I said. Mrs. Dibb says she was left badly off when her husband died, and I expect the money goes further here than it would in town. Besides, there's Bob. It wouldn't be so easy for him to get work.''

''A mischief-maker,'' said Bill hardly. ''If Cyril won't talk to her, Bess, I will. You don't want to take any notice—''

''Sit down, Bill, and don't talk rot,'' Antony advised him. Bill gave him a bewildered look and subsided again into his chair. Of the two of them, he was accustomed to being the leading spirit, and now he was surprised by the sudden decisiveness of the other man's tone. ''The important thing is, what is Bess going to do now?'' Antony went on. ''That's the problem, isn't it?'' he appealed to the girl.

''Yes. . . you see. . . I never thought it would cause talk, my staying at Stavethorpe Hall. Mrs. Clayton doesn't live in. . . but you know that. Only if people are saying. . . that. . . about Cyril and me, I don't see how I can stay any longer.''

''No, of course not.''

''I could go to a hotel in Great Allerton, but I dread that because I know people would stare. It isn't as if it was a big town where no one would know me. And anyway, the police told us not to go away until after the inquest. So I thought, just until then. . . with Mrs. Maitland here, *and* Mrs. Dibb, it could hardly be more respectable—''

''Of course you can stay,'' said Bill. He gave Antony a look as though he thought he might challenge the decision. ''It's the obvious thing to do.''

''Cyril doesn't think so,'' said Bess unhappily.

''Why not?'' Bill demanded. He still sounded truculent.

"He thinks I shouldn't take any notice at all of what Mrs. Clayton says. He says it's my home... well, it has been, of course. He thinks I should stay there. That's why I came away in rather a hurry and didn't bring anything with me, though I had packed a case."

"I can lend you a nightgown," said Jenny practically. "But he knows where you've gone, doesn't he?"

"I told him. I don't believe he thought I'd really come."

"Now that Hester's dead—" said Bill, and broke off as though he had just seen where the sentence was leading him. Antony completed it... it could do nothing but good, he thought, to set Bess's mind on the future.

"What are your plans? I agree, the immediate thing is to get the inquest over, and the funeral. But after that—"

"I suppose it sounds silly to say I haven't really thought about it. I think I took it for granted I'd just stay and keep house for Cyril. It's such a big house... even now I don't like to think of his being there alone."

"In the circumstances, it seems it can't be helped."

"He'll be lonely."

There didn't seem to be much to say to that. "Mrs. Thornton was your cousin, wasn't she?" Jenny asked. "have you any other relatives?"

Bess shook her head. "My parents were killed in the bombing at Hull. I only meant to stay at Stavethorpe Hall for a little while after I left school, and then look for a job. It's too far to go into town every day, unless you have a car, and obviously I couldn't afford that. But then Hester wasn't well, and seemed to need me, so I just stayed on."

"How long had she been ill?"

"Since... nearly a year now. She wasn't ill all the time, you know. It was just that she got these frightful bilious attacks, and they seemed to leave her weak. Now I think about it, the first one was early in May last year. I remember because she thought she was going to die, and she said she'd have liked to live until the blossom was out." She stopped and gave Jenny rather a misty smile. "I oughtn't to talk about it; I'm making myself cry."

"I'm sorry," said Jenny. "It would be better to think of something constructive, wouldn't it. Like what you're going to do."

"When all this is over I'll have to get a job."

"What sort of work?"

"I suppose I'm too young really to be anybody's housekeeper." Bess sounded regretful. "It would have to be office work, I expect. I don't really know what it entails, but I could learn."

"You'd have to live in town," said Bill. "You wouldn't like that."

"No, but... I don't see how it can be helped. I could be a land girl, perhaps, or a kennel maid, but I don't really think I should like that any better."

"Good God, no," said Bill, revolted. He seemed prepared to argue the point, and perhaps it was as well that Mrs. Dibb came in just then to see if she could serve supper. She took the news that Bess was staying in a matter-of-fact way that the girl seemed to find comforting.

"I'll just put clean sheets on your bed, Mr. Cleveland, then you can sleep down here on t'couch."

"I didn't want to disturb anybody," said Bess.

Bill started to say incoherently that of course he didn't mind, but Mrs. Dibb's flat, "That's all right, miss," was somehow more reassuring. They all ate their supper with good appetite, but perhaps it was as well that the phone call didn't come until the end of the meal.

Bill answered it. There seemed to be a good deal of talking going on at the other end of the line; they could hear a voice, but not what was said. After a while Bill said, "Yes, she's here; we're all agreed—" And then he was silent again until, "All right, I'll tell her," he said, and hung up and came back to rejoin the group around the fire. "That was Cyril."

"He's angry with me," said Bess in a hopeless way.

"With circumstances, I think." Bill was picking his words carefully, a thing he didn't often do. "I'm sure when he's thought it over he'll see what you did was the right thing."

"I don't know—"

"Don't worry about it, anyway."

"How can I help it?"

"He's coming over tomorrow sometime. He says he'll bring your case with him, so that'll save one of us a journey. I think you'll find he sees things quite differently by then." But Bess only shook her head.

Afterward, as perhaps was inevitable, they got back to the subject of Hester Thornton's death. It seemed that whatever they started to talk about led them in that direction, and finally Antony recognized the fact with a blunt question.

"You mentioned the police, Bess. . .that they wanted you to stay put until after the inquest. What exactly did they say?"

"It was just Sergeant Newbould. He came to see us last night after Hester died. You see, Doctor Todd said he couldn't sign a certificate, and that meant he had to notify the police, and the. . .the coroner. Sergeant Newbould didn't stay more than a quarter of an hour or so."

"Yes, but what did he say?"

"That there'd have to be an inquest, and we should both hold ourselves in readiness to attend." The words were obviously a quotation. "And then he wanted to know what Hester had had to eat or drink, but everything had been washed up, so that was no help. That was really all.''

"And quite enough," said Bill.

"More than enough," Bess agreed, with a movement of her shoulders that conveyed accurately enough her distaste for the subject. "More than enough, if Mrs. Clayton is to be believed."

"Don't think about that.''

"I don't see how I can help it. Besides, she said one funny thing, apart from what I told you."

"What was that?" asked Jenny, when it seemed that Bess wasn't going to go on without prompting.

"She looked at me in a queer sort of way, as if—as if we both shared a secret. And she said, 'There are more ways of killing a cat than choking her with cream.' I don't know what she meant."

"Nor does she, probably," said Bill in disgust.

Antony thought he did know, but if Bess was in the dark about it, he wasn't going to be the one to enlighten her. Nor did it seem necessary for Bill to know of the suggestion that witchcraft had been responsible for Hester Thornton's death.

# 5

IT WAS A LITTLE WARMER next morning, and the sky was overcast. Breakfast was at eight o'clock, and before that the milking had been done, and the pigs, who were inclined to be clamorous when hungry, had been satisfied. Antony burned his boats as soon as the meal was over by lighting the office fire; after that he was pretty well bound to use the room, under pain of Mrs. Dibb's displeasure. Outside, the routine work of the farm went on: Jenny was painting the barn door, Norman was boiling pig potatoes in the copper in the yard, which was harder work than it sounded, and Bill was sawing up some more of the discarded cattle stalls into lengths suitable for burning. Bess lingered indoors to help Mrs. Dibb with the household chores, but after a while she found another paintbrush, wrapped herself in an ancient tweed coat she found hanging up in the barn, and went to help Jenny. She seemed to be avoiding Bill. The two girls worked more or less in silence, but it was a comfortable, companionable silence, and Jenny was glad of the company. Besides, she had an idea that painting might be good therapy.

It was after midday dinner that the interruption came. Bill had gone to measure out the afternoon's feed for the pigs, Norman was in the dairy, and Jenny and Bess had finished the large doors of the barn and gone on to the small door at the side. As for Antony, he was still struggling to concentrate, but when he heard voices in the living room he went out, glad of the interruption, to see what was going on. If the weather was fine it wasn't often that any of the others were indoors, except at meal-times, until it was dark.

Bill had come in, and gone straight over to light the fire. The two men who followed him had an official air about them. The one in front looked small beside his companion: a thin man, with a sharp, ferrety face. The other was larger altogether, sandy haired, square faced, and with a placid expression. "Detective-Inspector Walton and Detective-Sergeant Holroyd," said Bill, straightening from his task. "Mr. Maitland, who is staying with me. They want to see Bess," he added less formally. "I'll send her in, but. . . why don't you stick around?"

"If Bess would like that." One year. . . nearly a year. . . of reading law hardly qualified him as an adviser, but he was not without experience of interrogation, from both sides of the fence, and that might be a help. Bill's voice had been flat and unemotional, but he clearly saw the implications of this visit and was alarmed by them. Antony went across to the fireplace and watched the flames leaping up among the wood. "Why don't you sit down?" he suggested. "I'm sure Miss Foster won't be long."

Neither of the two men availed himself of the invitation. For a moment they both regarded Antony in silence: a young man with clear gray eyes, a thin, intelligent face, and a casual, almost apologetic manner. Then Sergeant Holroyd cleared his throat and looked at the ceiling, while Inspector Walton said, not wasting time on nonessentials, "Is there any good reason, Mr. Maitland, why you should 'stick around,' as Mr. Cleveland put it?"

"Miss Foster is nineteen years old, Inspector.

Don't you think she might be glad of a friend at court?''

"And one of such age and experience," said Sergeant Holroyd ironically. He was still apparently inspecting the beams for woodworm.

"That's hardly the point, is it?" His tone was still mild. It would be hard to say where Inspector Walton got the impression that he was on the defensive. "Is there any good reason why I shouldn't remain?"

"None in the world," said Walton, with an expansiveness that didn't seem in character. "If that is what Miss Foster wants."

Bess came in at that moment, dropped the disreputable coat on the chair near the door, and came across the room to join them. Bill wasn't with her...perhaps that was wise of him. Antony effected introductions, watched Bess take the seat on the sofa that she had occupied the night before, which happened to have its back to the window. She was very pale, but more composed than he had expected, and she had a streak of green paint across her nose of which, almost certainly, she was quite unconscious. It did not occur to him that he was mentally labeling the two policemen as enemies and dangerous, which wasn't logical, because at the same time he was assuming that Bess had nothing to hide.

"Inspector Walton is going to ask you, Bess, if you would like me to stay."

"Bill said—" She broke off and rearranged the sentence. "Yes, please, Antony, I should like that."

"Then we'd better sit down." He joined Bess on the sofa; the other men took chairs at the opposite side of the hearth, and Sergeant Holroyd took out his notebook. The room was still cold, but the fire would soon take care of that. "How can Miss Foster help you?" Antony asked, instinctively feeling that the longer he could keep the initiative the better.

"It's about the late Mrs. Thornton," said the inspector. "There are a few questions—" But Antony wasn't ready yet to hand the floor over to Bess.

"Are we to take it, then, that you have had the results of the autopsy?"

"We have."

"And they are...?" He paused invitingly, and then said in a rallying tone, "Come, Inspector, if you are to ask questions you must lay the foundations, you know."

Walton looked at him with dislike. "Mrs. Thornton was poisoned with arsenic," he said. Bess gave a gasp of dismay, and said what was obviously the first thing that came into her head.

"How could that have happened?"

"That, Miss Foster, is what we want to find out. I am sorry to distress you—" he left the apology there "—but I must ask you to tell me what you can about her illness."

"Yes, of course," said Bess faintly.

"When was she taken ill?"

"About—oh, about ten o'clock on Saturday night."

"The doctor was sent for?"

"Of course," said Bess again. "He said...he thought...it was one of her usual attacks, only rather more serious than most of them. But I know he didn't expect—"

"Dr. Todd has told you all this, Inspector," said Antony.

"So has Mr. Thornton," said Walton. His tone implied, "What of it?"

"Then it can hardly be necessary—"

"You must know better than that, Mr. Maitland. It is always necessary to get what corroboration one can of every statement."

Which was true, of course. Antony made a gesture that conveyed his resignation of the point, without any particular pleasure. The inspector looked at Bess again. "What can you tell me about the course of the illness?"

"We were up with her all night, Cyril—Mr. Thornton—and I." Bess sounded almost matter-of-fact now, so perhaps the interruption had done some good after all. "She was violently sick, and at times she was restless and very thirsty. Once we thought the attack was over, she seemed quieter and more comfortable, but then it started all over again. Dr. Todd came in the morning; he promised to get us a nurse if he could. Then we sent for him again in the late afternoon, but before he could get there she died."

"Now we must go back to the Saturday evening. I want you to tell me, very carefully, everything that Mrs. Thornton had to eat and drink."

"I've been thinking about that," said Bess. "She had—we all had—sherry before dinner."

"That is, before your evening meal?"

"Yes, we always. . . Hester always liked to dine at night. We had chicken and ham and potatoes and cabbage. . . but I don't think Hester ate any of that. And afterward we had apple tart, but Hester had an egg custard I made for her; she didn't like to eat anything rich. And pastry can be so heavy when it's made with cooking fat on the ration, not with proper lard. And then we all had coffee."

"With milk and sugar?"

"With milk. Cyril is the only one who takes sugar."

"Who was in the house?"

"The three of us. And Mrs. Clayton. She stays until she has served dinner, and then she goes home and we wash up in the morning."

"Did she cook the meal?"

"Yes, except—"

"Except for the egg custard, which you made yourself."

"Well, I put it ready, just before we had our sherry. Mrs. Clayton put it in the oven when it was time."

"What ingredients did you use?"

Bess looked surprised. "Eggs, milk, sugar, a little butter. She didn't like things too sweet. And no nutmeg, because she thought it upset her."

"Can you suggest any way in which arsenic could have been added?"

That shook her. "No," she said. And again, more sharply, "No!"

"You're concentrating on the custard, Inspector," said Antony. The reason was obvious enough, but again he thought Bess needed a breathing space.

"It was the only thing—as I do not doubt you noticed, Mr. Maitland—that was not shared by the other members of the family."

"So it was," said Antony, with admiration in his tone.

Walton gave him a suspicious look, and Sergeant Holroyd said, breaking his silence, "Where did the eggs come from?"

"From the farm."

"How long had they been in the larder?"

"They were Friday's eggs. I know because Mrs. Clayton said we hadn't any left, and I went out to get them."

"You've been reading too many detective stories, Sergeant," Antony told him. "If you're thinking someone used a hypodermic—"

"We have to cover every possibility," said Holroyd, unruffled.

"And the milk?" asked Walton.

"From the farm, too."

"I meant, more immediately. It was kept in the larder, I suppose—"

"In a big white jug. I took what I needed—" Bess

was calm enough now, but she was frowning as she thought over her answer "—but I expect the milk we used for our coffee came from the same place, only it was poured into the cream jug first, of course."

"So we are left with the sugar."

"There's a tin in the kitchen where it's kept. I used some from there."

"And was the sugar basin also filled from this container?"

"I suppose so, but I don't know whether Mrs. Clayton had refilled it that evening or not."

"It would be interesting to know what Mrs. Clayton had to say about that," Antony said.

Inspector Walton eyed him in silence, but Sergeant Holroyd said helpfully, "The contents of the canister have gone to Wakefield for analysis."

"I see. Where do you suppose the arsenic came from?"

"If you remember, I asked Miss Foster—"

"Well, I can't imagine," said Bess, with more spirit than she had previously shown. "Mrs. Clayton always keeps the kitchen and the larder very clean and tidy. I don't think there's anything there that shouldn't be there."

"Do you know anything about a can of wood preservative kept in the cupboard under the stairs?"

"No...I don't think—"

"That's gone for analysis, too," Holroyd put in, in a pleased tone.

"I don't know anything about it," said Bess, with the wriggle of her shoulders that Antony had come to recognize as signifying distaste. "If it was in *that* cupboard, it couldn't have got into the custard, could it?"

"That remains to be seen," said Inspector Walton repressively. Antony half expected him to say, "I'm asking the questions," but if the words were in his mind he refrained from uttering them. "Now, Miss Foster, I should like you to tell me how long you have lived at Stavethorpe Hall."

"Two years in July . . . since a year ago last July, I mean. Before that I was away at school, and only here during the holidays."

"You were related to Mrs. Thornton?"

"Her cousin."

"Were you dependent on her financially?"

Bess flushed, but her voice was steady. "Yes, completely."

"On her, or on Mr. Thornton?"

"On both of them, I suppose."

"And now . . . do you think she will have left you provided for?"

"I don't know. I haven't thought about it."

"Was it a happy household?"

"Yes, very."

"No dissension between Mrs. Thornton and her husband?"

There was the slightest hesitation. "No," said Bess firmly.

"You don't seem too sure about that, Miss Foster."

"Of course I am . . . quite sure."

"How did you get on with Mrs. Thornton?"

"Why . . . well. I was grateful to her."

"No reason to feel . . . jealous of her, shall we say?"

"You've been talking to Mrs. Clayton," said Bess, her chin in the air.

"She has made a statement," Walton admitted.

"Well, I don't care what she told you . . . it isn't true!"

"Now, Miss Foster—"

Antony started to speak, but Bess interrupted him, saying quickly, "She said it's what people are saying. I don't believe it. Or if it is true, they've got evil minds."

"What are people saying?"

"That . . . oh, it's too silly," said Bess. Antony was in two minds whether to stop her, but as it turned out he was glad he hadn't. "I never thought of Cyril," said Bess scornfully, "except as a . . . a sort of an uncle." It sounded convincing. He found himself wondering if it was true.

At least for the moment it seemed to have satisfied the inspector. "May I take it that this gossip was the reason for your leaving Stavethorpe Hall?" he asked.

For some reason Bess did not answer immediately, so Antony said, to avoid the discomfort of a lengthy silence, "You can see it made an awkward situation."

"Thank you, Miss Foster," said Walton, ignoring him. Hearing the finality in his voice, Sergeant Holroyd shut his notebook and put it away. "What you have said will be typed out in the form of a statement, and I should like you to call at the police station to sign it next time you are in Great Allerton."

"That won't be until market day," said Antony, coming to his feet as the two policemen came to theirs. "At least, unless Mr. Thornton has more petrol coupons to spare than Bill has."

"Friday will do very well. You will be in town on that day in any case, Miss Foster, to attend the inquest, but you will be receiving notification about that."

"Sergeant Newbould told us—" said Bess.

"Formal notification," Walton told her. "Good afternoon, Miss Foster, and thank you for your help."

"I'll see you out," Antony offered, trying not to sound too eager. It seemed to him that it was the first useful thing he had said that afternoon.

## II

IT WASN'T YET TEATIME, but Jenny and Bill came in anyway, as soon as they saw the two policemen leave. Neither of them made the smallest pretense of not being interested in what had happened. "Hester was poisoned," said Bess, looking from one to the other of them as though anxious to see what they made of the statement. "They say it was arsenic."

"How . . . ?" said Jenny, and stopped.

"I don't understand," said Bess. "No one would kill themselves with arsenic, would they? And I don't see how it could have happened by accident."

"Do you think Hester might have committed suicide?" asked Bill.

"No, not really. She was often cross, but I don't think she was unhappy."

"Let's look in the encyclopedia," Antony suggested. "Have you got one, Bill?"

"Over there." Bill gestured toward the bookshelves on the left of the fireplace. "The fat, blue book on the bottom shelf." Antony went across the room to fetch it, riffling through the pages until he found the place he wanted. "Oh, Lord, there's masses of it," he said then, and there was a pause while he studied the closely printed page. "Here we are: 'Some wood preservative solutions sold for killing insects infesting wood are solutions of white arsenic (arsenious oxide), and as they are uncolored they are a source of danger.' Then it goes on with a lot of formulas. I don't think we need bother with those. If you can suggest a way, Bess, that the stuff could have got into the kitchen—"

"I can't."

"Well, never mind. I say, did you know that arsenic has been found in baking powder, caramel, vinegar, glycerine, jam, treacle, Demerara sugar . . . now, if that was what you used—"

"It wasn't."

"You can't buy it now," said Jenny.

"No . . . well . . . I expect there'd only be a trace in any of those things. It says here the fatal dose for an adult is generally two to three grains, and we'd all of us be dead by now—"

"I've just remembered something," Bess interrupted him. "Hester had a spoonful of gooseberry jam with her custard."

"And neither you nor Mr. Thornton . . . no, you were eating apple pie, weren't you?"

"Cyril doesn't like gooseberries, and neither do I."

"What about Mrs. Clayton? I expect she has some meals at Stavethorpe Hall."

"Yes, of course she does, and so does Bob. But I don't know anything about their likes and dislikes."

"Still, it might be a good thing to tell the police. What do you think, Bill?"

"I'd like to know what *they* are thinking."

"They think I did it. Or perhaps Cyril, but most likely me," said Bess with a shudder.

"That's absolute rot."

"They haven't exhausted the possibilities of accident yet," said Antony in a placatory tone. "I really think we should tell them. I mean, they might find that Mrs. Clayton kept some of her preserves in the cupboard under the stairs, as well as the wood preservative, and that would be a step in the right direction."

"I'm sure she wouldn't do such a thing," said Bess, shaking her head. "For one thing, we have an enormous pantry."

"Even so . . . we can ring the police station when they've had time to get back to Great Allerton. I suppose that's where they came from."

"It is," said Bill. He still sounded angry.

"Then it can't do any harm to show willing. Unless, of course, Mr. Thornton has told them already." And at that moment, as if on a cue, Cyril Thornton rapped on the door and came in without waiting for an invitation—a man of medium height, slightly built, with fair hair and rather cold blue eyes. He was carrying a small suitcase, which he put down before approaching the group around the fire.

"There you are, Bess," he said. "I'm sorry I couldn't get away before." That he was under a strain was evident as soon as he spoke, but that, thought Antony, wasn't to be wondered at.

Bill got up. "These are the Maitlands, Cyril. Jenny and Antony. Antony has been lending Bess his moral support—"

"Have the police been here, then?" asked Thornton sharply.

"They only just left. I'm surprised you didn't meet them."

"There was a car that I didn't recognize coming down the Edge. But I hoped I'd get here—"

"It didn't matter," said Bess simply. "I couldn't tell them anything. . . except the truth."

"What did you think I wanted you to tell them?" Thornton asked roughly. "I only didn't want you to be upset." He broke off and ran his fingers through his hair. Then he turned to Jenny and said with a smile that transformed his rather austere features and made him immediately more likable, "I'm forgetting my manners, Mrs. Maitland. Forgive me."

"We were so sorry," Jenny said sedately, "to hear of Mrs. Thornton's death." She looked up and caught Bill's eye and colored faintly, because she knew the words were banal, but what else could she say?

Cyril Thornton said, "Thank you." And then added with a short, unamused bark of laughter, "It's beginning to look as if we ought to say, 'her murder.'"

There was a brief, appalled silence. Jenny looked down at her hands, Antony turned to throw more wood on the fire, Bess said, "Don't!" in a voice that sounded strangled.

Bill, when the pause became unbearable, said gruffly, "Is that what the police think?"

"What else?"

"Antony felt they were still considering the possibility of accident."

"If I thought there was any chance an accident might have happened. . . I don't, I'm afraid."

"Then you believe—"

"I don't believe she killed herself, if that's what you mean."

Antony turned from the fireplace. "The trouble about murder," he said guilelessly, "is. . . who did it? Has your Mrs. Clayton a motive, I wonder."

"No conceivable motive."

"She got on well with Mrs. Thornton?"

"Well enough."

"A financial motive, then."

"No. Hester made her will when we were married. . . we both made them at the same time. I'm the sole beneficiary."

"I see. But I don't suppose your kitchen is an impregnable fortress. Did you tell the police about the gooseberry jam?"

"Jam?" said Cyril, startled.

"Hester had some with the custard I made," Bess explained. She looked up at Antony, still standing on the hearth rug a little to one side of the fire. "Do you really think the arsenic might have been in that?"

"If you and Mr. Thornton are known not to care for it—"

"But that would mean someone we know."

"If you won't accept either accident or suicide—"

"Neither makes sense," said Cyril abruptly.

"No . . . well . . . I don't suppose it was a homicidal maniac, do you?"

"I see what you mean." This time Cyril sounded thoughtful. "Someone with a motive for wanting Hester dead. But no one could have wanted to kill her."

"Suppose for a moment there was such a person. Who could have had access to the larder, or kitchen cupboard, or wherever the jam was kept?"

"I don't know."

"Someone who was watching for an opportunity, and had nerve enough to take it when it offered. What about it, Bess?"

"Almost anyone who called might have been in the kitchen at some time or other," she said slowly. "If it was during the day, when Cyril was out and Mrs. Clayton had gone home for a while and Hester was lying down, perhaps, it would be quite natural for a visitor to come into the kitchen with me while I made a cup of tea, or something like that."

"Yes, of course. Can you remember any recent visitors?"

"I . . . it's like accusing them, isn't it?"

"Not really."

"Pretty well all our neighbors have called at one time or another during the last month," said Cyril, less scrupulous than Bess. "Ronald and Daphne Undercliffe walked over from Burntside Hall one Sunday; and Wilfred Damerel calls quite frequently, and Micklefield has been over on farming affairs once or twice, and that generally ends with our going into the house for refreshment; and I know Fay Dodgson often calls in to see Mrs. Clayton on her way back from market; and your Mrs. Dibb, of course."

"And me," said Bill. Thornton acknowledged the

interruption with a rather tight-lipped smile and went on without hesitation.

"Other visitors—friends from Leeds or Rothershaw—come more formally, to dinner, and would have no opportunity . . . but all this is nonsense, of course."

"The police might not think it was."

"Well, I've no intention of telling them," said Cyril shortly.

"I'm sorry," said Antony, answering the tone rather than the words. "I know all this is in the worst of taste, but I do really think it might be helpful to get things clear in your own mind. If Bess is going to tell the police about the gooseberry jam, and I think she should . . . have you any idea how long it was since it was last used, by the way?"

"I shouldn't think very long," said Bess. "It was . . . she was very fond of it. I don't remember exactly, I'm afraid."

"Do you know when it was bought?"

"It was homemade. The Damerels' housekeeper made it, and Margot brought it one day last year when she came to see us."

"After the gooseberry season, I suppose."

"August, I think. Or it might have been September."

"I see."

"I still think it's all nonsense," said Cyril aggressively. "No one had any reason—"

"It might be interesting to know," said Antony, putting forward the suggestion with an appearance of diffidence, "what Mrs. Clayton told the police."

"All the gossip, I suppose," said Cyril, angry again.

"They must have questioned her also on matters of fact."

"I daresay."

"They seemed to be interested in the sugar."

"Yes, they asked her about that. I know, because she repeated all that part of the interview to me at some length."

"Well?"

"The sugar bowl hadn't been refilled for several days, but she had used some out of the canister when making the apple pie. I don't see how that helps us at all."

"When did she make the pie?"

"Saturday morning," said Bess, looking bewildered.

"There must have been something more to her evidence than that."

"There was, of course. A great deal about her feelings."

"Where was she while you were drinking your sherry before dinner?"

"Between the kitchen and the dining room, she said. Setting the table, I suppose." He waited a moment, as though resigned to further questions, and then turned to Bess with one of his tight-lipped smiles. "Are you coming home with me?"

She looked at Jenny, as though seeking counsel. "Nothing has changed," she said in a low voice, "since last night."

"I suppose you haven't thought that you're giving the neighbors something else to talk about." His voice was ragged again, reflecting the tension that he tried so hard to hide. "Rushing away like that. Anyone would think you were afraid of me."

"You know why I came away. It's best for both of us."

"I don't agree with you." He shrugged his shoulders and then came to his feet. "Well, if you won't come back, you won't. There's nothing I can do about it." He made for the door.

"Cyril—" said Bess, and waited until he turned

and looked down at her. "I'm doing what I think is right. Don't make it any harder."

His expression softened. "You know I only want what's best for you, my dear. But sometime we've got to think of the future."

"Not now," said Bess. "Not yet."

"So long as you understand you've nothing to worry about."

"I'm not worried about *that*."

"Very well, then." For a moment he remained, his eyes fixed on her face, then he turned to Jenny. "I should be thanking you, Mrs. Maitland."

"There's nothing to thank me for," said Jenny warmly, though she was wondering why he had this effect on her, that all her remarks sounded, in her own ears, trite and commonplace. But perhaps, after all, it was circumstances, not the man himself.... "We're all very glad to have Bess here."

"Then I'll be going."

"It's nearly teatime," said Bill.

"I won't stay, thank you. Everything's at sixes and sevens today and I ought to get back." He lingered a moment, then raised his hand in a general salutation and made purposefully for the door. As he pulled it open there came the sound of squealing from outside, as the young pigs gathered at the field gate to demand sustenance.

Jenny got up in a hurry. "It's past feeding time."

"We'll do them now and then have tea," Bill decided.

Antony took one look at Bess and saw the tears in her eyes. "I may as well come and help you," he said, and followed them out.

**6**

IT WASN'T OFTEN that Antony helped with the feeding. The fact that he could only carry one bucket at a time brought him face to face with his disability, which wasn't a position he enjoyed. There were too many memories bound up with it. This evening, however, it seemed the line of least resistance, though he would have been hard put to say how honest he was in thinking that Bess would rather be left alone.

It was already growing dark, and the air had a damp feel about it, very different from the hard frost of the last few days. Cyril climbed the gate, made his way with difficulty through the assembly of pigs, and started up the field. Bill came out of the barn with a bucket in each hand, and the squealing rose to a crescendo as he approached the gate. "They've shut us in here and left us to sta-a-arve," said Jenny, smiling at Antony as he came up with her. He was horrified to find himself ruffled by her evident pleasure in his company, because he thought immediately, she thinks it means I'm getting back to normal. . . whatever normal is; but he stifled the feeling as well as he could, and was able to respond quite amiably when she went on, "That Tony-pig is a perfect fiend."

"I didn't know I had a namesake in the farmyard."

"He isn't called after you, he's Saint Anthony's pig, because of being the runt of the litter," said

Jenny, lucidly for her. "You'd never think it now, would you? He even bites Curly, who only wants to sleep all day, to make him squeal, too. I always think if there was a revolution here—like the book, you know—he'd be leading it. I can just see him with a machine gun, manning the barricades."

"I'd no idea they had such dangerous potentialities."

"Darling, you sound exactly like Uncle Nick."

"Do I? Never mind." He surveyed the row of buckets. "What do you want me to do?"

"The two on the right are for the field. If you take them as far as the gate you can pass them over to Bill. The other one is Grunter's. I'd better take that myself, because she knows me."

"She seems an amiable enough animal," said Antony, picking up one of the buckets.

"Yes, but she's nervous. Did Bill tell you she hasn't got a squeal?"

"I thought all pigs—"

"Not Grunter. She has a fine turn of language when the spirit moves her, but no squeal."

"I wonder if her progeny—"

"It's an idea, isn't it? Perhaps with line breeding. . . Bill might become quite famous." They were outside again by this time, and Jenny turned left toward the farrowing pens, while Antony went across the front of the house toward the field gate. He had made the two journeys, and was filling a bucket from the tap in the yard, when Norman came out of the mistal with another stockier man behind him, and Laddie, of course, in attendance.

"You'll not have met Seth Dodgson, Mr. Maitland."

"No, but Mr. Micklefield mentioned him, I think." He put out his hand (you shook hands in Thorburndale), and it was taken in a firm, almost painful grip. At a second glance, Dodgson was so broad shouldered as to be almost square; he had a craggy, weather-beaten face, and hair that must have been sandy once, but now was brindled.

"That's right. I work for him," he said. "Glad to meet you, Mr. Maitland. I'm just on my way back from Great Allerton." Norman quietly took up the bucket and went down to the gate where Bill was waiting for it. "You must like these parts to be staying here at this time of the year."

"I do, very much indeed."

"Most townsfolk say, 'It must be lovely in t'summer.'"

"I expect it is." What was the matter with him that he could think of nothing to say beyond the bare agreement?

"You ought to visit us, then. Mr. Cleveland could do with a hand, with t'hay and all. This time of year . . . well, it's quiet like."

"Restful," said Antony, and thought how very far that was from being the case.

And, as if he had read his mind, Dodgson went on, "Not but what we're having our share of excitement, what with Mrs. Thornton getting herself poisoned." Dodgson was eyeing his companion a little too closely, as though hoping to surprise him into some unwary expression of opinion. "And now," he added deliberately, "they've had trouble over to Burntside."

For some reason it was important that he shouldn't show his sudden interest. "That's the house near How Gill, isn't it?" said Antony casually.

"Aye. Undercliffe's place."

"What happened there?"

"Prowlers," said Seth Dodgson succinctly.

"That doesn't sound very alarming."

"Stands to reason they're up to no good."

"I suppose not. But what evidence—?"

"First it was t'barn door left open. He didn't think much of that, Mr. Undercliffe didn't, just that he'd been mistaken, thinking he'd shut it. But then on Sunday night he heard quite clearly that someone shut the gate between the garden and what used to be t'farmyard, and when he got to door there were two men getting into a car that went off up t'lane."

"What were they like?"

"Just shadowy figures, Mr. Undercliffe said." Dodgson sounded pleased with the phrase. "It wasn't all that light, you know, even though there was a moon." (I remember, I was out, too.)

"What time was this?"

"Nigh on eleven."

It was a measure of his previous uneasiness that now he was aware of an almost overwhelming sense of relief. At least he hadn't been imagining things that night in How Gill. Nor had it been witches, unless, he thought with sudden amusement, the modern variety had abandoned their broomsticks, and enjoyed a quiet cigarette sometimes in the intervals of their ritual. "Someone after the chickens, perhaps," he suggested.

"They don't have any stock. Mr. Undercliffe would have it they were planning a burglary, proper upset he was, but I don't see it myself. Why would they be in t'farmyard, if that was what they wanted?"

"Why, indeed? Could it have been someone who lost their way?"

"Not likely. There's a gate at top of t'lane with name of t'house. Nothing to make them think there was a way through."

"They must have come from the moor road, then. The one from Great Allerton to Beckwith."

"No other way, not by car." He moved away a little, to the low wall that bounded the kitchen

garden. The ground fell away steeply here, so that
when Antony joined him they were both standing
looking out across Thorburndale. "Nobbut a mile
and a half on foot, if you take track down to
t'packhorse bridge," Seth explained. "But by car
it'd be nearer eleven miles. . . six into Great Allerton, and then out by t'Beckwith road."

"And yet they're one of our nearest neighbors. It
makes you think," said Antony tritely. "It's the
same with Dallow Park, isn't it? Their only way out
by road is over Monkton Moor."

"That's right. Easier to walk, especially these
days, with petrol rationing and all. You've done
some walking yourself, I hear. . . when you're not
shut up with your books."

"It makes a change." It was Fay Dodgson, wasn't
it—this chap's wife—who had told the Micklefields
of the rumors that were circulating about Bess
Foster? It was easy to see where she got her information. Dodgson had a ready tongue and a trick of
silence that invited confidences; it would be the
easiest thing in the world to fall into a gossiping
conversation with him. "It's good country for walking."

"It is that. Well, I'd best be getting along," he
added as Norman came back to join them. "I stopped by at Stavethorpe Hall on my way up
t'Edge. . . Fay had a recipe she wanted me to pass
on to Martha Clayton. So I'm a bit behind."

The two of them moved off together, leaving Antony standing, looking out across the darkened
valley. His thoughts were far away, and he was
startled out of all reason when Bill came up beside
him, silent in his rubber boots, and spoke without
warning.

"Penny for them."

"Damn you, do you have to creep around like
that?"

"I can't help it," said Bill mildly. "Somehow I don't see myself in clogs." He waited a moment and then went on, "I made you an offer."

"A penny for my thoughts? They're not worth it." His mood had changed again, and his tone was bleak. Bill eyed him curiously.

"You seemed very preoccupied."

Perhaps because for an instant he had been genuinely afraid, for once he spoke what was in his mind without evasion. "I feel as if I shall never be of any use again to myself or to anybody else."

"That's a bit daft, isn't it? What about this afternoon?"

"What about it?"

"First there was the police—"

"You could have looked after Bess as well as I did. Better, perhaps." (Without antagonizing that fellow Walton.)

"I don't think so," said Bill. "Then there was Cyril...your talk with him opened up all sorts of possibilities. You seem to know instinctively what to ask." He paused, and then added tentatively, "I suppose it isn't so different from the kind of thing you were doing during the war."

It was the nearest Bill had ever come to questioning him. "There's no comparison at all," said Antony shortly.

"Isn't there? I should have thought...but then, you've never told me, have you?" He broke off, and there was a little silence. A wind had got up that rattled the branches of the larch tree; from the field came a soft, wuffling sound as the pigs finished their supper. Norman had lighted a storm lantern and gone into the house with Laddie, leaving it hanging on the bracket outside the kitchen door. "Why will you never talk about it?" said Bill.

"Because...oh, because." Though he didn't realize it, his mood was a natural progression from the effort he had made to speak lightly to Jenny, and the still greater effort it had needed to allow Norman to complete a job that he himself found difficult to do. Even so, he might have left it there, but he was angry suddenly: with Bill for his insistence, but more than that with himself. "Heaven and earth," he said with barely suppressed violence. "Must I remember?" Bill started to say something, but he swept on unheeding. "It sounds good, doesn't it? Intelligence work. But there's no glamour about it, no dignity...only squalor."

It was quite dark now; he could no longer make out Bill's features, couldn't see if he was looking concerned or (intolerably) sympathetic. But, just for the moment, he was past caring. "If you're caught—" he hesitated a moment and his voice hardened "—there's none of the decent drama of being shot at dawn. *Möchten Sie eine Zigarette, mein Herr? Haben Sie Feuer?* All that went out a long time ago. You may get a knife in the back and die in the gutter...not much romance in that. Or they may want to ask you questions. You'll die just the same, most likely. It's only if you're very lucky that you live...to look back on it. Emotion recollected in tranquillity." He laughed. "That couldn't be more unapt."

This time the pause was a long one. "I...see," said Bill at last. And then, "You've never really come to terms with everyday living, have you?"

"That's one way of putting it." There was a queer kind of relief with which he was not at all familiar in saying what was on his mind, but he couldn't have done it to anyone but Bill; certainly not to Jenny, who cared so terribly. "The thing is," he added in a tone that was almost casual, "I think I've lost my nerve."

"I don't believe it for a moment."

"Don't you? Perhaps it doesn't greatly matter." He let the silence lengthen again, and it was Bill who broke it.

"This business of reading for the bar—" he was going carefully, feeling his way "—are you sure it's the right thing to do?"

"It's what we planned, what I wanted to do before. . . I don't see why I should let *them* change my mind."

"I thought you were finding it a bit difficult to settle down."

"I am. That isn't the point, is it?"

"Perhaps not. Anyway, I wanted you to know, if you do have second thoughts about it, I could do with a partner." Antony turned his head sharply. "There's even a place we could build," Bill went on, "near the gate onto the Edge opposite Ram's Syke."

"If you need a partner, Bill, get one with two good arms," said Antony, but now there was only a tinge of bitterness in his tone.

"It wouldn't matter—"

"It would to me. Not that I'm not grateful."

"Don't be more of a fool than you can help," Bill urged him.

"I've a sort of feeling—" He stirred and looked around. "Never mind. Has Jenny gone in, do you suppose?"

"Five minutes ago. Tea should be ready."

"Then what are we waiting for?" His voice sounded quite normal now—a little flat, perhaps, in the aftermath of emotion. He turned and made for the kitchen door, but when he came into the circle of lamplight he stopped and looked at Bill. Then, seemingly satisfied with what he saw, he went into the house.

II

As it was so late, Mrs. Dibb had combined tea
and supper into one high tea, an enormous meal, at
which one of her own stand pies was the pièce de
résistance. Afterward Jenny came through from
the kitchen with a Kilner jar about one-third full
of cream, which she proposed to shake until it
separated. Both Antony and Bill were quite used
to this ritual, in which they participated in turn
when her arms grew tired, but Bess eyed the
project with obvious bewilderment. If she had
been crying there was now no sign of it, but there
was a lethargy about her movements, as though
the afternoon's events had been more of a strain
than she would admit. "What are you doing that
for?"

"Don't you make butter?" asked Bill. "I thought
everybody did who had even a drop of milk to
spare."

"Yes, of course, but we have a little churn."

"That's all very well, but you can't buy a churn
now for love nor money. I know . . . I've tried."

"Everything's so difficult now, isn't it?" said
Bess, sighing. But somehow Antony didn't think it
was purely postwar problems that were in her
mind.

Cyril Thornton phoned about half an hour later,
and Bill took the call. His own part in the conversation was unrevealing, and they all waited in
silence for his explanation when he came back to
the fire.

"He asked Mrs. Clayton about the jam."

He didn't attempt immediately to add anything
to that, and after a moment Bess said with some
impatience, "Of course he did. What did she say?"

"That she'd never eaten any of it. She doesn't
like it, either."

"Was that all?"

"Not quite. She found the jar empty, and washed it up with the dinner things on Sunday morning."

"So there's nothing to show—"

"I still think you should tell the police," said Antony.

"It's so inconclusive," Bess protested.

"Yes, but—don't you see—nobody thinks much of the chance of an accident at your end, but such a possibility might exist at Dallow Park, for all we know. If the poison was in it all along, that might account for the bilious attacks Mrs. Thornton suffered."

"Yes, well. . . wouldn't it do if I told them on Friday?"

"Now," said Antony inexorably. "Tonight. Bill will do it for you."

"If it were Sergeant Newbould," said Bill. "But I don't know this Walton chap. It would come better from you."

"Walton doesn't like me." They argued a little longer, but in the end it was Bill who went to the phone. The inspector wasn't in, as it happened, but he left a message at the police station in Great Allerton. When he rejoined the others Antony was on his feet.

"I'm going for a walk," he announced. "Anybody coming?" But the suggestion was a half-hearted one, and he wasn't surprised when they all declined the invitation.

It was overcast tonight, but once his eyes grew accustomed to the darkness he managed well enough. He made the longer circuit: to Winterscale and across the bridge there, and back along the footpath at the other side of the river as far as Riddingstones, where he crossed again and so came home. A cattle truck passed him opposite Ferrens

Point, and he thought briefly, though rather vaguely, of Constable Lister and his problems. He lingered a while in How Gill, and even walked up beside the barn until he could see the back windows of Burntside Hall glowing through the darkness. But all was silent except for an owl that hooted sadly in the wood, and after a while he went on his way again. He usually found that exercise stimulated his mind, but tonight it didn't seem to work. . .or perhaps it worked too well. His thoughts were chaotic; he couldn't seem to get them in any order at all.

So he came down the Iron Age track and climbed the six-barred gate that was tied down because Grunter was quite capable of lifting it off its hinges if she felt so inclined. He went along quietly as far as the sty, and lifted the sacking over the peephole so that he could peer in. In the light of the storm lantern it was a warm, comfortable scene: the little pigs asleep in a heap in the corner under an infrared lamp, fenced in so that Grunter couldn't lie on them, and the sow herself stretched out on the clean straw, dead to the world and breathing deeply. A comfortable scene, and somehow comforting in its promise of stability in a changing world. He dropped the sacking into place again and started toward the house, moving a little stiffly as he always did when he was tired and the nagging pain in his shoulder more insistent than usual. But as he passed the barn he noticed that the door was open, and before he had time to do more than think that Bill must be on his evening rounds, he heard the sound of movement and then, unmistakably, a groan.

Bill was on the ground just inside the doorway. The flashlight he had been using was still in his hand, and Antony took it and shone it around the interior of the barn, but there was nothing to be seen, nor did anybody seem to be around outside. He went down on one knee then, and took a look at his friend, shading the light with his hand, and Bill opened his eyes and said, ''Where...what...what the devil—?''

''What happened?''

''Oh, it's you.'' Bill struggled into a sitting position and put his head in his hands. ''Somebody slugged me,'' he said. ''Did you see...?''

''There's no one around now. How long have you been lying here, for heaven's sake?''

''No idea. I came out...about half-past ten,'' said Bill jerkily.

Antony flashed the light onto his wristwatch. ''It's five to eleven now.''

''Well, I'd been out for about ten minutes when it happened, I should think. All quiet...didn't hear anyone...didn't see anyone. Just stuck my head in here to see if the cat had kittened yet, and that was that.''

''What do you suppose—? Let me have a look at your head.'' He used the flashlight again. ''There's a lump the size of an egg,'' he reported, ''and a jagged cut...you're a bit of a bloody mess.''

''You're telling me,'' said Bill with feeling.

''I was wondering what they'd used.''

''There are plenty of bits of wood lying around. What does it matter, anyway?''

''It's just that...that stone, for instance. It'd make a nasty sort of weapon. I tell you, Bill, I don't like it.''

''In confidence,'' said Bill, ''neither do I.''

''I mean, there's a viciousness about it. Well, you can't go on sitting there. Do you think you can get up?''

''Of course I can. The top of my head may fall off,'' he said as he scrambled to his feet, ''but apart from that—''

"Good. They had prowlers at Burntside Hall a couple of nights ago," said Antony as they moved toward the house. "Did you hear about that?"

Bill didn't answer that directly. "There couldn't be any connection . . . or could there?"

"That's anybody's guess. The police may have some ideas about it."

"I suppose we've got to call them. Twice in one evening seems excessive."

"Yes, but . . . I think we must, don't you?" But when they got into the house and Antony went to the phone while Bill told the girls what had happened, he found the line was dead.

"So that's that. Tomorrow is also a good day." He wasn't altogether sorry for the postponement. It was late, and he was tired, and sleep would probably do Bill more good than anything else.

"He should see the doctor," Bess objected.

"For a little thing like this? Nonsense," said Bill. "There's some iodine in the bathroom cupboard." But Jenny was already halfway up the stairs.

When she came back with disinfectant, cotton wool and a bottle of aspirins, Antony said, "I'll leave you to your Florence Nightingale act and get Norman and have a look around outside." He was a bit surprised that Laddie hadn't barked, but Norman said they were both used to hearing Mr. Cleveland moving around at night, and in any case he was a working collie, not a guard dog. This was misleading; Laddie was affectionate and enthusiastic, but not particularly good with stock.

Now they all three of them searched carefully, but they didn't find any trace of an intruder, except the place where the telephone line had been cut and a length of the cable removed so that it couldn't easily be joined up again, which confirmed Antony's surmise but wasn't really helpful.

### III

"I DIDN'T WANT TO MAKE A FUSS," said Jenny, when they were alone in their bedroom half an hour later, "but I do hope Bill will be all right."

"He will be, love. Take my word for it."

"They might have killed him."

"Easily, if they'd wanted to. As they didn't, we must assume he was merely temporarily in their way. And when I say 'they,' one man behind the door would have been sufficient."

"I don't like things I don't understand," said Jenny. And then, changing the subject in a determined way, "I never had a chance to ask you, Antony. Did the police know what people are saying about Bess?"

"They knew all right."

"Everything?"

"They didn't mention the witchcraft bit, of course. That would be to make fools of themselves. But the trend of their questions—"

"What did Bess say?"

"The best thing she could possibly have done. She said she looked on Thornton as an uncle."

"Nieces have looked on their uncles with affection before this," said Jenny, sitting down in front of the dressing table and picking up her hairbrush.

"If you mean what I think you mean... such cynicism, love."

"I didn't—" She broke off, and sat staring raptly at her reflection as though she had never seen it before. "Oh, well... perhaps I did."

"I thought you liked Bess."

"I do. I don't see what that has to do with it. She doesn't *have* to be in love with Bill."

"No, of course not. But in the circumstances it might be convenient—"

"I don't think you ought to think of Bill as a . . . a sort of alibi." Antony laughed.

"We're going around in circles, Jenny," he said, and sounded now more relaxed than he had been all day. "Open the window, love," he added, "and come to bed."

7

HE WALKED ACROSS to Stavethorpe Hall immediately after breakfast the following day to telephone the police. He was connected with Sergeant Newbould, who received his report phlegmatically and promised to come and see Mr. Cleveland later in the day. He also called the telephone company, who said they would send someone to repair the damaged line, but they did this without enthusiasm, and he judged—rightly as it turned out—that they wouldn't be in any great hurry to do so.

Cyril Thornton was still at the breakfast table when he arrived, and offered coffee as soon as he turned away from the telephone. Antony agreed, because he got the impression the other man had something on his mind, but all Cyril asked when his visitor was seated was, "How's Bess this morning?"

The answer to that seemed to be the hospitals' stock bromide. "As well as can be expected. She's worried, of course," he added, and wondered as he spoke why his tone sounded defensive. "I don't see how you can expect anything else."

"I don't," said Thornton, and gave a laugh that sounded very far from amusement. "I couldn't help hearing what you were saying on the phone just now," he went on abruptly. "What's all this about someone attacking Bill?"

Antony told him, as briefly as possible.

"Is he badly hurt?"

"He has a sore head, but he's all right this morning. Not even a headache, or so he says."

He wasn't at all sure that Thornton was listening to him. "Makes you wonder what's going on in Thorburndale, doesn't it?" he said. "You heard what happened at Burntside Hall?"

"No one was hurt there."

"No, but still. . . . The police were here asking questions about the black market," said Cyril. "Do you think there might be any connection?"

"I don't see. . .if there had been a pig missing now, but they were all present and correct at roll call this morning. And the Undercliffes don't have any stock, or so I'm told."

"No, I suppose. . .it's a puzzle, though, isn't it?" He laughed again, self-consciously. "It's a relief, really, to have something else to think about besides what happened to Hester."

There wasn't much to be said to that except a plain agreement. "Things may seem clearer after the inquest," Antony said awkwardly. And then, "The police have been told about the gooseberry jam, and where it came from."

"Do you really think that will help them?"

"I don't see why not."

"Because I don't suppose Damerel's housekeeper is any less meticulous than Mrs. Clayton is."

"Not knowing either of them—" Antony finished his coffee, which hadn't been very warm to start with, and got to his feet. "I mustn't keep you," he said.

"No hurry. It's a dead time of year. Would you like to have a look around the farm?"

"Very much." He wasn't in any hurry himself, and glad enough of the excuse not to return straight away to his books. Thornton, poor chap, must be pleased with anything that took his mind from his own problems.

"We'll go out the back way." Antony followed. No one seemed heartbroken about Hester Thornton, no one had expressed more than a conventional sorrow at her death, but surely in her lifetime the house hadn't had this dead feeling, as though all the life had been drained from it. The kitchen was better, spotlessly clean and almost too tidy, but at least there was a certain amount of activity going on. He was introduced to Mrs. Clayton, a little, dour-looking woman with bright, inquisitive eyes, and then they were outside and he was aware of relief, though he couldn't have told what caused it.

Unlike Brass Castle, which was surrounded by its buildings—jostled by them, as it were, on every side—the farmyard at Stavethorpe Hall was behind the house, a completely separate entity, with its own gate onto Stavethorpe Edge. There was the Fordson Major tractor, blue and red, and bigger than Bill's orange-colored one, which Jenny called Dutch William, and some rusting pieces of farm machinery in a corner, whose purpose was not immediately apparent to Antony's untutored eye. There was the barn, as old as the house, or nearly, and the mistal and dairy, comparatively new, with a dozen nice-looking Friesians, eight of which—Cyril said—were in milk. There was the largest haystack he had ever seen, and some brown hens scratching near the midden. Then there were the piggeries, old buildings converted. "You don't let them run out, then?" said Antony, watching a gawky youth—Mrs. Clayton's son, perhaps—forking muck out of the end sty.

"No, it's different for Bill; he's breeding. Pays him to keep his sows fit and to be on good terms with them. I buy weaners and fatten them...that lot there are from Brass Castle.

They'll be ready to go to the factory in about three weeks' time.''

"I see. Wouldn't do to get fond of them.''

"It's just a job," said Cyril, "like any other. You're reading law, aren't you? Well, it wouldn't do much good for you to worry unduly about your clients, I don't suppose.''

Uncle Nick would say the analogy was far from perfect. "I don't suppose so, either," said Antony vaguely.

"A hellish way of earning your living," said Cyril, with some of the abruptness he had shown before.

"The law?''

"No, farming.''

"Bill seems to like it.''

"He hasn't got over his first enthusiasm." He hesitated, and then asked, "How is he getting on?'' The casualness of his tone was rather over-done.

"Very well," said Antony, warily. He felt the same stir of uneasiness that had affected him when he was talking to Professor Micklefield two days before. "I'm not an expert, of course," he went on, trying to pass the question off lightly, "but it doesn't seem to me there are more than a normal number of crises at Brass Castle.''

Thornton laughed again. "You're quite right. Farming is largely a matter of living from one crisis to the next. After a time it begins to pall.''

"I suppose so," said Antony in polite agreement. He was thinking, if things were going badly for Bill he'd tell me, wouldn't he? On the other hand, he offered me a partnership; a friendly gesture, or something more...a need for more capital, per-haps. If I said I wanted to go farming, what would Uncle Nick say? Something scathing, doubtless, but might he not secretly be glad? That was an uncomfortable thought, and he put it aside for later consideration. Bill wasn't a devious character, he didn't really believe he'd go about anything in such a subtle way, but if he was up against it financially that might make a difference.

"You can take it from me," said Cyril, breaking in on these reflections, "if it weren't for Bob Clayton—" he gestured toward the gawky youth, who was just disappearing around the end of the barn with his wheelbarrow "—I don't know how I'd get on."

"He's a good worker?"

"Good enough, but a bit dim. Not a bad thing, really; he doesn't waste time chattering. Only when Seth Dodgson's here, he'll hang around waiting to have a word with him. I don't know what the attraction is."

"Some common interest...pigs, perhaps," Antony suggested.

"Perhaps," Cyril agreed. "Well, that's the whole operation, except that I have a hundred sheep gaits on the moor."

"They shouldn't give you much trouble," said Antony, with a vague notion of having heard of dog and stick farming.

"There's lambing and shearing and time to cull the flock," said Thornton, obviously not in agreement with him. "If it isn't one thing it's another." He turned away, and added with an air of finality, "That's all. Not much to show for all the work."

"It's very interesting," said Antony, not altogether truthfully. There was nothing obviously wrong here, but a subtle air of neglect that made him uncomfortable, an atmosphere of frustrated hopes. He made his farewells rather hastily, and breathed more easily when he came out of the farm gate onto the Edge. After a brief struggle

with himself he turned up the hill to take the short
way home.

II

SERGEANT NEWBOULD was a majestic, ginger man.
He arrived soon after dinner, leaving the ancient
Austin with the "clue trunk" parked in High Lane.
Antony did not hear his arrival, and it was only
when he was summoned by Mrs. Dibb that he put
on his pullover and went out to find him standing
with Bill near the barn door. Neither Jenny nor
Bess was anywhere to be seen. "The scene of the
crime," said Bill as he came up. "Sergeant Newbould is baffled."

The sergeant didn't appear at all put out by this
somewhat unceremonious introduction. He said,
"Good afternoon," and favored the newcomer
with a piercing glance that made Antony thankful
that he had a clear conscience, at least as far as
any misdemeanors that might interest the police
were concerned. "Well, now," said Sergeant Newbould comfortably. "It'll be you as found Mr.
Cleveland, so he tells me."

"That's right."

"What time was that?"

"About five to eleven." He liked the policeman
instinctively, but at the same time was aware of
his own, equally instinctive recoil from the turn
the conversation was taking. There had been a
time when there were too many questions. . . .

"And what were you doing out at that time of
night?" asked Newbould. He seemed quite unaware of anything odd in the atmosphere.

"Bill had been—"

"I meant yourself, Mr. Maitland."

"Taking a walk." He couldn't help it, he could
hear the hostility in his own voice, though he

knew quite well the sentiment was both foolish and unnecessary. Not surprisingly, Sergeant Newbould gave him another of his sharp looks, though his tone remained friendly and unruffled.

"There's not many people care to be out after dark at this time of year for pleasure."

"It was overcast, but not really dark when you got used to it," Antony explained.

"Constable Lister tells me you're a great one for walking."

"Does he, indeed?"

"Where did you go last night?"

"Across the bridge at Winterscale and back by Riddingstones."

"That's a fair walk."

"Fair."

"Did you come up the fields, or around by Stavethorpe Edge?

"By the Edge and along High Lane and down the track." He gestured as he spoke.

"So you approached the barn from the gate there."

"Yes."

"Did you see anything or hear anything?"

"Only Bill. He gave a sort of a groan."

"Nowt else?"

"Nothing."

"And on your walk, did you see anybody around?"

"Not a soul." He hesitated, and then corrected himself. "At least, there was a truck passed me just as I got to the end of High Lane and started down the hill."

"Did you notice anything about it? The owner's name painted on the side...the license plate," suggested Sergeant Newbould hopefully.

"Nothing like that. And it wasn't parked anywhere around when I came back."

"It's a right puzzle, Mr. Maitland, isn't it now? Mr. Cleveland tells me nothing had been disturbed."

"So I understand."

"How did you think he had been injured?"

"I thought...that stone." He was surprised by the question. "Something jagged, anyway. Not a sandbag, or a cosh."

"I wouldn't wonder if you're right." The sergeant bent over and examined the piece of rough stone that Antony indicated. "Looks like blood," he said, nodding. "I'd best be taking it along." He produced a large handkerchief and plopped the stone into it, holding it by the corners, and began to move away toward the gate. "You're from London, Mr. Maitland, if all I hear is true."

"I am."

"An old friend of Mr. Cleveland's."

"I've known him all my life."

"That's nice," said Newbould, looking from Antony on his left hand to Bill on his right. "Would you be knowing, then, of anybody who had a motive?"

"Your province, Sergeant, not mine."

"Ah, well." He sighed. "We like to get what help we can, Mr. Maitland, but if you don't know—"

"I don't." He meant to leave it there, and was astonished to hear himself amplifying the statement. "It was a...a matter of convenience, knocking Bill out. Not malice."

"How do you make that out?"

"I didn't disturb the chap who did it. I didn't come along until about ten minutes after he was hit. Plenty of time to do considerably more damage, if that was the object of the exercise."

"Yes, I see. I'll have to take your word for that, Mr. Maitland." They had come to the gate now, and Bill was untying the piece of rope that lashed it down. Sergeant Newbould thanked him, thanked them both for their cooperation, and set off up the track with the long, deceptively slow stride of the countryman.

Bill watched until he was out of sight, and then asked mildly, "What was that in aid of?"

"I don't know what you mean."

"You didn't exactly fall over yourself to be helpful."

"I don't like answering questions," said Antony shortly.

"That was sufficiently obvious."

"Well, I'm sorry. I liked your Sergeant Newbould—"

"Did you though?" said Bill skeptically.

"Yes, I did." He turned and leaned his back against the gate, and gazed past the farrowing pens to the garth at the back of the house where a number of pigs were disporting themselves. "What do *you* think happened, Bill?"

"I haven't the faintest idea."

"I was right, wasn't I? Nobody has a grudge against you."

"You know as well as I do—"

"Not necessarily."

"There's something on your mind." Bill sounded exasperated. "You'd better tell me."

"The same idea that had occurred to the good sergeant, unless I miss my guess. They're investiga-a-ting the black market—" unconsciously he drew out the word in the local accent "—and if somebody had made an approach to you, and been turned down—"

"Do you take me for a fool? I'd have told you."

"That's what I thought." Antony's tone was bland. Bill laughed reluctantly.

"You'd infuriate a saint," he said. "But if it'll

make you any happier I'll deny it categorical-
ly: nobody has approached me, as you put it, so I
haven't had a chance to turn them down. As a
matter of fact," he added thoughtfully, "I'd be a
very bad prospect for a deal like that."

"Why?"

"I haven't any beef. If I get a bobby-calf it goes
to market at the first opportunity. As for the pigs,
I never have more than a couple of hogs fattening
for our own use; otherwise there are just the
breeding sows, and their litters are sold as
weaners. If I started fattening for the black market
it would be perfectly obvious."

"To any instructed eye."

"To Sergeant Newbould and Constable Lister, at
least."

"I see. Whereas if Cyril Thornton, say, diverted
some of his fat pigs—"

"Not too fat," Bill objected. "They're
baconers."

"Yes. . . well. . . whatever. If he diverted some to
the black market, it wouldn't be obvious at all."

"It would take some proving, certainly."

"Also he has some sheep, he told me. Who's to
say if one or two go missing?"

"What are you trying to prove?"

"Nothing at all. I'm trying to broaden my mind.
Which of your other neighbors could get away
with it?"

"I only know Micklefield and Damerel. It's quite
ridiculous to think—"

"For my edification."

"Oh, very well," said Bill. "Damerel has some
beef stirks, but he sends them down to fatten at
one of his farms in Ellerdale. He has some sheep; I
don't know how many. Also some hogs for fattening; he's had some of my weaners, as Cyril has. He
is, I should say, a moderately wealthy man."

"Very suspicious," said Antony, with intent to annoy; but this time Bill refused to be drawn.

"Micklefield breeds pigs...sells the gilts in pig and fattens the hogs himself. He has no beef, but quite an extensive flock of sheep, I believe. You could make quite a good case out about either of them on the strength of their stock."

"I'm not trying...but you must admit it's interesting. For instance, Professor Micklefield could hardly indulge in any nefarious activities without Dodgson's knowledge, but Dodgson might quite well have a racket going on the side...don't you think?"

"I suppose he might," Bill admitted grudgingly. "But there's nothing to show that Thorburndale's involved in any way."

"Only that it's one of the most sparsely populated districts—"

"That works both ways. Strangers are pretty noticeable; you know that yourself."

"Yes, there's that. But something's going on."

"I reckon nowt to the Burntside Hall prowlers," said Bill, falling in his turn into the local idiom. "Someone who'd lost their way."

"Do you really think so?"

"What else?" His tone was challenging, but Antony didn't answer, so after a moment he went on, "As for what happened to me—"

"If you've got an explanation of that I'd like to hear it."

"Well, I haven't. But it wasn't malice...you said that yourself. And it wasn't black market."

"I think you're right," said Antony seriously.

"Do you, indeed? It didn't sound—"

"There's another queer thing happened in Thorburndale that we can't very well ignore. Hester Thornton's death."

"That's an isolated incident...nothing to do with anything else."

"No?"

"Of course not. Besides, it was an accident...it must have been," said Bill positively.

"We don't know yet what the poison was contained in."

"Don't you think the jam is the best bet? If Damerel's housekeeper—"

"She'd have to be pretty careless. Now if it had come from the bank manager's household—"

"What have you got against bank managers?"

"Nothing personal. Uncle Nick says they're a godless race of men."

"If you can't take it seriously—"

"I can. I do."

"It's not a very nice thing for Bess. Or for Cyril, either."

"He doesn't like farming," said Antony irrelevantly. But Bill declined the gambit, and presently went back to the barn to put up the evening rations. Antony lingered a moment, but it was nearly teatime, a good enough excuse not to go back to his books, so he thought he might as well go in.

Jenny was alone in the living room. She had lighted the fire and was curled up in one of the big chairs listening to a Toytown play on the Children's Hour. Antony went and stood with his back to the hearth, warming himself, and exchanged a smile with her as Dennis the Dachshund spoke earnestly to Frau Goose. Come to think of it, Sergeant Newbould had something in common with Ernest the Policeman, insofar as they both were worthy upholders of the majesty of the law. It would be nice, though, if life were so simple.

The radio was an old-fashioned one that stood on a table in the corner, and ran off a car battery to which it was attached with crocodile clips. Cheaper that way, Bill had said. But it was one thing to have to watch every penny, which was only to be expected when you were plunged suddenly into the postwar world, sink or swim, and without any worldly experience to buoy you up; it was quite another to be really up against it financially, to be faced with the prospect of having to give up the life you'd dreamed of, probably, for years and years. He thought again, Bill would have told me... but how could he be sure? He ought to have asked him point-blank, of course, but that was one of those things that are easier said than done.

## 8

FRIDAY WAS MARKET DAY in Great Allerton, and a bus with the name Murgatroyd painted on the side went down from Thorburndale in the morning, and came back at four o'clock in the afternoon. Jenny had been down on it the previous week, and spoke well of its amenities: not only the human passengers, but a crate of hens, a calf in a sack with just its head showing, a little pig, similarly attired, but not quite so philosophical. Antony and Bill, meanwhile, had taken the van with a dozen importunate piglets in the back, all of them with the ambition, or so it seemed, to climb out of the back and sit on the driver's knee.

That Friday, however, there was no stock to be conveyed, so they took the car and all four went down in comparative comfort. Bill had an old Austin, not quite so venerable a vintage as Sergeant Newbould's, and much more rakish in its lines. It stormed the hills willingly enough, but there were disadvantages on a wet day; the roof leaked and the floor admitted a sort of tidal wave on the passenger side whenever it went through a puddle. That day, however, the rain still held off, though it was rawly cold and there was a stiff wind blowing.

The inquest on Hester Thornton was scheduled for eleven o'clock. Jenny and Bess, armed with Mrs. Dibb's list, went off to the shops. Bess was subdued that morning, and even quieter than usual, though she hadn't exactly been hilarious company

# FREE
# to RAVEN HOUSE.

MAIL THIS CARD TODAY!

## Four **FREE** books for you

MAIL TO: **Raven House Mysteries**
1440 South Priest Drive, Tempe, Arizona 85281

**YES,** please send me FREE and without obligation my 4 Raven House Mysteries. If you do not hear from me after I have examined my 4 FREE books, please send me the 4 new Raven House Mysteries every month as soon as they come off the presses. I understand that I will be billed only $2.25 per book (total $9). There are no shipping and handling, or any other hidden charges. There is no minimum number of books that I have to purchase. In fact, I may cancel this arrangement at any time. The first 4 books are mine to keep as a FREE gift, even if I do not buy any additional books.

RCI01

Name                    (Please Print)

Address                                    Apt. No.

City

State                                        Zip

Signature    (If under 18, parent or guardian must sign.)

This offer is limited to one order per household and not valid to present subscribers. Prices subject to change without notice. Offer expires December 31, 1982.

**MAIL THIS CARD TODAY FOR YOUR 4 FREE BOOKS**

during the past few days. And no wonder, thought Antony, mentally rebuking himself for the implied criticism. He watched them go, until all he could see in the crowd was the red knitted cap and the blue one, and then turned to follow Bill from the car park to the square, where the bank was situated.

The Northumbrian and Wessex Bank had a corner site, and was an imposing building for so small a town. Bill's business didn't take long—a couple of checks to deposit, and a small withdrawal—but as he was turning away a man came out of a door at the end of the counter and greeted him cheerfully. "Just the man I wanted to see." Antony, who had been strolling across to join his friend, retreated again to one of the desks by the wall, with nothing to amuse him but a supply of deposit slips and withdrawal forms, and Bill followed his captor back through the door into what was presumably the manager's office.

They emerged again about five minutes later, and this time Bill signaled to Antony to join them. "Antony Maitland," he said, "who is staying with me. This is Mr. Undercliffe, Antony, who is the manager here." He sounded as calm as ever; there was no telling, thought Antony (who was still frankly jittery on the subject of Bill's finances), what the interview had been about.

Undercliffe was a small man with dark, sleek hair and a toothbrush mustache. There was no real resemblance, but you might draw a caricature of him and have it taken for a representation of the late Adolf. He was wearing tweeds, but even so he didn't succeed in looking like a countryman. He said, "How d'you do?" formally, and then, in a more friendly tone, "You're the young man who walks."

"So does everybody else in Thorburndale."

"Yes, but only on business."

"It's an odd thing," said Antony, "I never seem to meet anyone, but all the same—"

"Nothing ever goes unremarked in the country. I've just been asking Cleveland here about his adventure."

"It's a puzzling thing, isn't it?" No harm, perhaps, in turning the tables a little. "I hear you had some excitement yourself."

"Somebody prowling around the place. No harm done. And that's a puzzle, too."

"Someone who had missed their way." (Who had suggested that? Even as he spoke he knew it didn't sound likely, not from what he'd heard.)

"It couldn't have been that on Tuesday night," said Bill.

"No, it would have been rather an extreme reaction—"

Undercliffe came with them to the door. Antony felt his cordiality was a trifle strained, and wondered again what had passed between him and Bill, but perhaps it was his natural manner. They came out again into the square. Bill wanted some things from the hardware store, but Antony had an errand of his own in mind.

"Have you got your library ticket with you?"

"Yes, do you want it?"

"If you don't mind. I thought I'd try to get hold of that book by Clough that Professor Micklefield mentioned."

"I'll see you at the café, then, in about ten minutes' time."

The county library was in Moorgate, next to the White Boar, its Victorianism making an odd contrast to the simpler lines of the older building, though both were of the local stone. Inside it was rather dark and extremely crowded; whatever had been the original plan it was obvious that more and more stacks had been added, until you could only

make your way around between the shelves of
books if you were reasonably in training and kept
your weight down. Antony found an assistant and
gave her what information he had, wishing at the
same time that he had thought to ask the professor
to be more explicit, but she said immediately,
"Clough's *History of Ellerdale and Thorburndale*.
It's funny you should ask for that."

He smiled at her. "Why is it funny?"

"Nobody reads it now. Old-fashioned, I expect. I
don't know when we were last asked for it, and
now...twice in a month—"

"Don't tell me it's out."

"It came in last night. I haven't had time to put
it away yet." She produced it from a curtained
recess under the counter, a heavy book in an un-
distinguished brown binding. "There!" she said. "I
hope you enjoy it."

"I'm sure I shall." He hesitated. "Do you remember who had it out before?"

"Yes, I do." She was puzzled for a moment, but
obviously, when she thought it out, she saw
no harm in the question. "It was Mr. Sweeney.
I noticed because it was a change for him; he
usually takes out thrillers, spy stories, things like
that."

"I wondered if it was one of our neighbors in
Thorburndale."

"Oh, no, Mr. Sweeney lives here in Great Allerton. Leeds Road," she added, as though this somehow made the statement more credible, and went
on to give him a word of advice. "Don't go taking
all Clough says as history, though, for all that's
what it's called."

"No?"

"He was not always discriminating in his choice
of material," she said, leaving Antony to wonder
whom she was quoting.

"But legend can be just as much fun as fact...
don't you think?"

"So long as you know the difference," she told
him seriously, and he went away reflecting that this
was sometimes easier said than done.

Turning back into the square again, he saw Bill
crossing from the other side, his arms full of
awkward-shaped parcels. They met on the pave-
ment, and had turned in the direction of Betty's
Café, which was over the drugstore on the corner,
when they heard someone calling, "Mr. Cleveland," and stopped to allow a youngish, tallish man
in a duffel coat to come up with them. "Haines," he
said, a little out of breath. "You remember me, Mr.
Cleveland, at the auction."

"Yes, of course," said Bill. "When I bought Brass
Castle," he added to Antony, and seemed to think
that was introduction enough. "Nice to see you
again." If he was at all puzzled at being accosted,
he hid it very well.

"Well, I thought...seeing you like this...I
thought there was no harm in asking," said Haines,
still breathing rather fast.

"If I knew—"

"Sorry. Not explaining properly." He took a deep
breath, and started again. "Whittington and
Haines, Estate Agents," he said, as if that made
everything clear. Antony thought for a moment of
Jenny, who wasn't good at explaining things,
either, but then his attention was caught by something odd in Bill's tone.

"I remember that...of course."

"No harm in asking," said Haines again. "Heard
you were thinking of selling...glad to handle
things for you."

"Who told you that?" asked Bill. Probably only
someone who knew him as well as Antony did
would have realized that he was growing angry.

"Don't remember exactly." That might have been true, or it might have been a belated instinct of caution. "One of your neighbors, as far as I recall."

"Well, they told you wrong," said Bill rather abruptly. "It's no use discussing it; I've no intention of selling . . . now or later."

"Sorry I spoke."

"It doesn't matter." Bill turned away, and Antony paused only to smile at Haines, who was looking rather dejected, before following him. He was still a couple of paces in the rear when they came to the drugstore. "I'll just leave these things here," said Bill, making a detour into the shop and depositing his purchases in an already crowded alcove, along with a number of shopping bags and baskets, all more or less full. If he was at all put out by their recent encounter, he wasn't showing it.

"That's all very well," Antony objected. "How can you be sure of getting your own again?"

"It seems to work," said Bill. But Antony went upstairs to the café with his book still tucked under his arm.

The girls hadn't arrived yet, but they ordered coffee straightaway, because time was getting on. "People!" said Bill as soon as they were alone together. "How do you suppose that story got around?"

"That you want to sell?"

"Yes, of course," said Bill impatiently, and went on, without waiting for a reply, "That's the second person this morning."

"Who—?" asked Antony, but he thought he had a very good idea.

"Undercliffe. They haven't a mortgage on the property, you know . . . that's with the Huddersfield Mutual. But he wanted to point out that if I sold Brass Castle the bank would require immediate repayment of my overdraft."

"I see."

"It's reasonable enough, I suppose, from his point of view. I told him there was no question. . . I don't know if he believed me. But somebody must be spreading the story, and I'd like to know who it is."

"It doesn't take much to start people talking," said Antony carefully. "I've wondered myself— only, of course, I shouldn't say so to anybody—how you are doing."

"Things will be tight for a year or two. That's no more than I expected. . . nothing I can't cope with."

"That's good," said Antony, taking care to hide his relief. Bill would either avoid the subject altogether or tell him the truth, he knew that well enough. "It must be a pretty solid rumor for Mr. Undercliffe to have spoken to you, let alone that fellow Haines. But, as long as it doesn't cut off your credit with the bank, it can't do any harm that I can see."

"I suppose not," said Bill in a dissatisfied tone. "But then, there's this talk about Bess. . . that's much more serious. I thought it was just Mrs. Clayton being spiteful, but I don't see what she could know about my affairs."

"If people have a mind to talk, I don't think they need to *know* anything. It will pass," said Antony, and was glad to see Jenny and Bess coming across the room to join them. He didn't really want Bill to see how uneasy all this gossip made him. Particularly the small, added malice—which surely nobody could believe—of the story that Bess was a witch.

II

THEY DRANK THEIR COFFEE hurriedly, and Bess was fidgeting all the time because Cyril Thornton hadn't arrived to meet them, as arranged. Finally they had to leave because of the inquest. Bess had to attend, of course, and she seemed to want Jenny with her; Bill wanted to go, but Antony was of two minds about it...he had a nasty feeling that whatever they learned they might wish they hadn't. But in the end it seemed easiest to go along with the others. They met Cyril at the bottom of the stairs on his way up to find them.

The hall where the inquest was to be held was in Bridge Street, another ugly gray building, with the words Mechanics Institute engraved in stone over the entrance. The room to which they were directed was large and dusty, and about as uncomfortable and cheerless as a room could be. It was also well filled with people. Cyril and Bess were ushered to chairs near the front, and neither of them looked at all happy with the distinction. The rest of the party found places near the rear wall, Antony and Bill standing, and Jenny being given a seat by a boy who looked as if he ought to be in school.

And, after all, the proceedings lasted barely twenty minutes. The coroner was a big, taciturn man, a local solicitor, Bill said. He heard evidence of identification from the husband of the deceased; medical evidence that confined itself strictly to the cause of death and the amount of arsenic found in the body; and a request from the police for a fortnight's adjournment, so that they could pursue their investigations, to which he acceded with every appearance of pleasure. They found themselves out in Bridge Street again almost before they realized it. There were a lot of people around, but they took up a position near a lamp standard and let the crowd swirl around them.

"Nothing," said Antony, "about how the poison was administered."

"There's no secret about that, Mr. Maitland," said a voice behind him. "We don't know." He turned to find that Inspector Walton had come up with them, with Sergeant Holroyd in attendance. The inspector had a pleased, almost a smug look about him.

Antony looked around quickly, but neither Cyril nor Bess was yet in sight. He said, "If I've got it right, it was either in the jam or the sugar," and made the words a question.

"The sugar," said Walton, "was clean."

"And you've no means of knowing about the jam. How disappointing for you." If the inspector was in a forthcoming mood, there was no harm in taking advantage of it, but Antony suspected his motives.

"No means at all," Walton agreed. He turned his head a little to look at Bill. "You've been having some trouble yourself, Mr. Cleveland, from what I hear."

"Nothing serious, I'm glad to say." Jenny exclaimed reproachfully when she heard this, and Bill gave her a reassuring smile.

Walton said, "Quite right, Mrs. Maitland, a nasty thing to happen."

Sergeant Holroyd added in his deep voice, startling them all because of his previous silence, "Mysterious."

"Have you any theory about the motive, Mr. Cleveland?" Walton asked.

"None at all."

"If this were a storybook, now, it would be a simple matter."

The inspector still sounded bland, and he looked from one of the young people to the next rather as if he was a schoolmaster awaiting the answer to a test question, so that Jenny said, as if she felt impelled to make some reply, "The least suspicious person."

"Or the person who found him," said Walton. "You'd qualify on both counts, wouldn't you, Mr. Maitland?"

"Admirably. I'm sorry to disappoint you, though... if I'd wanted to knock Bill out I shouldn't have used a stone." Antony sounded amused.

But when the inspector went on smoothly, "You were a commando during the war, perhaps?" his answering denial could hardly have been more curt.

"No," Walton echoed, and looked again from Antony to Jenny to Bill. "You'll remind Miss Foster about signing her statement, won't you?" he said, and turned away. Sergeant Holroyd lingered only a moment to say, "Good morning," before he followed.

"And what," said Bill as soon as they were out of earshot, "do you make of that?"

"He was joking," said Jenny uncertainly. "Wasn't he?" she appealed to her husband.

"Getting a bit of his own back, love. I succeeded in annoying him the day he talked to Bess."

Bill said thoughtfully, "He thinks the better a person knows me, the more likely he is to hit me over the head."

"Precisely," said Antony, amused again.

"That's only because he doesn't know you very well," Jenny said consolingly, so that both the men laughed, and had to break off abruptly when they saw Bess and Cyril making their way through the crowd to join them.

Bess was looking pale and shaken, and said in a despairing tone without preamble, "Nothing's settled. And I thought it would be all over today."

"It can't be helped." Thornton's tone had the roughness that Antony had begun to recognize as a cover for some emotion. "I suppose the police know their own business best," he added without conviction.

Jenny was silent. You couldn't go on saying, "I'm sorry." It didn't help; in fact it only served to underline what you were trying to forget. Antony and Bill started together, "The police—" and both broke off to allow the other to complete the sentence.

Cyril said impatiently, "We don't need any reminding. This ridiculous business of the statements. I suppose we'd better go now and get it done."

"We're in the car park," said Bill. "When Bess is ready—"

"Don't wait. I'll bring her back myself after lunch. There are things," said Cyril, "that we have to talk about."

"Yes, of course." It wasn't often Bill sounded at a loss, but he did now. "We'll see you later, then, Bess. Anytime you like."

Their ways lay together until they came to the ginnel, known locally as Lily's Back, that led to the car park, but they parted there without anything else at all being said. Bill tried to enliven the drive home with the story of Jacob Wood, who had been seen returning from the market one day the previous year with his three sons in the trailer with eight "old yows," while the lambs rode in comfort in the back of the car. "It's noan so easy to addle brass," he had said bluntly when asked about this reversal of the usual order of things, "and lambs costs money." And then, in biblical vein, "Any fool can get sons." But somehow none of them now was in a mood to be amused.

### III

ANTONY SHUT HIMSELF INTO THE OFFICE after lunch, pushed his law books ruthlessly to one side, and set himself to study the one he had brought from the library. Mr. Clough's style was a little pompous, a little given to the carefully rounded phrase, but his subject matter was full of interesting things for all that. But when Antony looked for Burntside Hall in the index, and turned to page 436 in response to what he read there, he found that the page, and the one next to it, had been carefully cut out.

There was nothing to tell, of course, whether it was Mr. Sweeney of Leeds Road, Great Allerton, who had done it, or whether it was some earlier reader.

He told Bill and Jenny about it at teatime. Bess still hadn't returned, and Bill didn't refer to the fact, but he seemed uneasy. "What did you want to know about Burntside Hall, anyway?" he asked.

"What Clough had to say about the treasure."

"Why so interested in that?"

"The local history," said Antony vaguely.

"Well, I daresay Micklefield could tell you. He may even have a copy of the book himself."

"That's an idea. I suppose Mrs. Dibb didn't say if they'd been yet to repair the phone."

"Not yet."

"I'll walk over in the morning," Antony decided.

"I still don't see... you're not beginning to believe in this story of buried treasure, are you?"

"I might be," said Antony, doing his best to look enigmatic.

Bill eyed him consideringly, and then said slowly, "Well, I'll be blowed."

Jenny, who had been concentrating on the pouring out, looked up from her task. "I think it's a wonderful idea, but why?" she said.

"It isn't so much that I believe in the treasure," said Antony, deciding to explain, "as that I think somebody else may. Suppose this *History* of Clough's gave some particulars of where it was rumored to be hidden at Burntside Hall."

"The prowlers," said Bill, enlightened. "But that's a bit farfetched, isn't it? They wouldn't be treasure hunting in the dark."

"A preliminary survey. To see if they could identify the location, to see if there was a dog that barked...that kind of thing."

"But even then...unless they were sure of the precise spot, then I suppose they could do something."

"I know what I'd do in their place."

"What, for instance?"

"Make inquiries in Great Allerton. Find out which day Mrs. Undercliffe goes shopping, when the maid has her day out...if they have a maid. That sort of thing."

"It would need a good deal of nerve to go digging up the place in daylight, even so."

"But think what's at stake. Something that could be referred to as treasure in the seventeenth century would be fabulously valuable today."

"If it exists at all."

"As you say. But—"

"The whole idea's fantastic."

"Fantastic, yes, but not impossible." He paused, but Bill continued to look skeptical, and less good-humored than usual. "I'm only trying to explain what happened," said Antony persuasively, "first at Burntside Hall, and then here."

"For heaven's sake!"

"Yes, but it isn't all that unreasonable," Antony told him. "They're not local men—not Thorburn-dale, that is—but by some means or other they hear of the legend."

"It's the sort of thing the local papers might bring up from time to time," said Jenny.

"So it is. I must remember to ask Micklefield about that."

"He'll think you're mad," said Bill, not mincing matters.

"That can't be helped. Anyway, grant that they've heard the legend. Grant, too, that they're keen to take any chance of making money, and not too worried whether the method is legal or not.''

''But—''

''If they'd just been interested—from a historical point of view, or whatever—they wouldn't have had to go about their researches in a clandestine way.'' Antony was pressing on without giving Bill a chance to formulate his protest. ''So, grant all that. Like sensible men they take their problem to the local library—at least, one of them does, a chap called Sweeney. And there it all is, in black and white. . . the story that the treasure is buried at Burntside Hall. Don't you think they'd go and look?''

''They might.''

''You're not giving me much encouragement, are you?''

''Do you need any?'' asked Bill sourly. ''Are you trying to tell us that by looking around at night they satisfied themselves it wasn't at Burntside Hall, after all?''

''No, I think that between Sunday night, when someone was seen there, and Tuesday night, when some unauthorized person was certainly here, they heard the more persistent local rumor and transferred their attentions to Brass Castle. I also think— and I'd be the first to admit I'm guessing—that their informant may have been Seth Dodgson.''

''Why on earth?''

''He was in Great Allerton on Tuesday afternoon; he told me so when he called in here on his way home. He's a gossipy sort of chap—''

''Is he?''

''Oh, yes, I think so. Also, he knows the legend as well as anyone. . .he used to live here. Did he own the place, Bill, or was he the tenant?''

''As far as I recall from the deeds, he owned it. It was only a small holding then. When he sold it in 1940 the new owner bought another seventy-five

acres or so from Cyril Thornton...all the Stavethorpe Hall land that lay on this side of the Edge."

"That's interesting. I wonder why Thornton
sold."

"What the hell does it matter why he sold? He
told me once, as a matter of fact," added Bill grudgingly, "that it was because he was short of capital."

"Well, that's reasonable enough." He paused,
smiling. "Don't you like my hypothesis?"

"Pure fantasy."

"I'm not wedded to it," said Antony meekly.

"I should hope not. Anyway, while you're so
busy explaining things, how did it help the treasure
hunters to hit me over the head?"

"They retreated before you...one, or more of
them, there's no means of telling."

"Can't you even make a guess?"

"I would, if there was anything to be gained by
it," Antony retorted. "Let's say it was just one
man...Mr. Sweeney, perhaps. He takes shelter in
the barn, but you go in there, too, and start flashing
your torch about...what else was the poor chap to
do?"

"It's nice to know the whole thing was my own
fault."

"I wouldn't say that. Not altogether," said Antony thoughtfully.

"Well, why haven't they been back?"

"Because they know we're on the alert. They
want to lull us into a sense of security."

"*I* don't feel insecure. This nonsense of you coming around with me at night, for instance—"

"A commonsense precaution," Antony assured
him. And then, "Bear with me, Bill. You must admit it's a better explanation than anything you've
been able to think up. Or the police, for that matter."

"You don't know what they're thinking."

"I can guess. . .sorry, you don't like the word, do you? If they couldn't think up any better theory than that I did it, I'd say they were baffled, myself."

"All right, I'll grant you that," said Bill, his stiffness melting a little. "And I must say I'd like to hear you propounding this theory to Inspector Walton. But I can't see anybody being so silly as to waste their time—"

"Professor Micklefield and his band of enthusiastic helpers gave up a summer to it. Remember?"

"But they were working quite openly—"

"That isn't the point. They thought there was, at least, a good chance the treasure was there, or there'd have been no point in the operation."

"I see what you mean," said Bill, but he didn't sound altogether happy. "Give me some more tea, Jenny," he added, "and let's talk about something else."

Jenny followed him, willingly enough, into speculation as to the possible fertility of Huff and Puff, the two gilts from Grunter's first litter, but Antony was lost in his own thoughts. He was rather more serious than he sounded about his theory, and a good deal more worried. He couldn't forget that his whole instinct that night in How Gill had warned him of danger.

IV

BESS CAME IN AN HOUR LATER. They were all in the living room: Bill studying the *Farmer's Weekly*, Jenny diligently hemming a sheet that Mrs. Dibb wanted turned "sides to middle," Antony turning the pages of Clough's *History*—which seemed to have suffered no other mutilation—and occasionally reading aloud some passage that struck him as good value. Bess looked tired, but she had a little

more color than usual. Bill gave her his place by the
fire, and said as she seated herself, "We were
wondering where you were."

"I'm sorry. I tried to phone, but it's still out of
order. I went home with Cyril for a while."

Whatever any of them said, it would sound like
curiosity. . . and they were curious, that was the
trouble. There was a difficult little silence, and
then Bess went on, "We decided I should go home
during the day. . . will you mind if I do that? And
just sleep here at night, for the time being."

She was looking into the fire, and the question
didn't seem to be directed to anyone in particular.
Bill said, too heartily, "You must do as you like,"
and Antony, eyeing Bess more closely and seeing
something stubborn in her expression, thought to
himself, she means to, and then wondered a moment later—when she spoke again and he heard her
troubled tone—whether he had been wrong about
that.

"It's using you like a hotel. I'm sorry." She was
looking at Bill now, asking for his understanding.
"There are things I can do; the house is too big for
Mrs. Clayton to manage, and besides, I don't think
it's good for Cyril to be too much alone just now."

"It's a difficult time for both of you," said Jenny,
looking up for a moment from her seam.

Somehow this not very original remark seemed to
strike a responsive chord in Bess. She said, much
more naturally, "He's awfully worried, you know.
About Hester. We both thought the police would
find out what had happened, and it would be all
cleared up at the inquest today. But now it seems as
if they don't know anything more than we do."

"Did they explain why they asked for the
adjournment?"

"They said to allow them time to proceed with
their inquiries."

"An official way of saying they're stymied," said Bill.

"Yes, I should think so," Antony agreed. "Did you sign your statement?"

"We both did, but they didn't really *say* anything, you know. I don't see how they could help the police. And Inspector Walton asked me all over again what happened the day Hester was taken ill, and then about the jam, but I couldn't tell him any more than you had done already, Bill. Just that she had it."

"The thing is, did he tell you anything?"

"That wood preservative—"

"Yes?"

"It did contain arsenic. In fact, they said it was a solution of white arsenic. It could have been what was used."

"It *could* have been," said Bill, taking what encouragement he could from emphasizing the word. "Did they say anything more than that?"

"No, only . . . there was one other thing."

She hesitated and looked appealingly at Jenny, and Jenny said encouragingly, "You may as well tell us, Bess."

"Yes . . . it was only . . . she'd been taking arsenic on and off for several months."

"Then it was the jam," said Bill triumphantly. "An accident at Dallow Park . . . a horrible thing to happen," he added, awkwardly, suddenly realizing that his tone wasn't altogether appropriate to the subject, "but nothing anyone could help."

"That must have been it," said Bess, and fell silent again, looking down into the fire.

# 9

Bᴇss ᴡᴇɴᴛ ᴏᴜᴛ sᴏᴏɴ ᴀFᴛᴇʀ ʙʀᴇᴀᴋFᴀsᴛ the next morning, but for decency's sake Antony lingered a little before setting out for Ferrenscross. He took a book into the kitchen to avoid lighting the office fire when he'd only be there for an hour or so, but Mrs. Dibb, who didn't really approve of all this reading, was in a talkative mood, and he didn't get much done. He thought she was worried, but when he considered the matter afterward he wasn't quite sure what this conclusion was based on. It was colder this morning, but also brighter than it had been for the last few days, and Jenny had gone back to her paint cans again.

Professor Micklefield seemed pleased to see him, and offered him coffee and some of Daisy's scones. Antony was getting used to the casual hospitality of the country now, which wasn't always possible in town with rationing still in full swing, and accepted with pleasure. They went into the professor's study, and he explained his problem. "The pages I was interested in are missing, so I was wondering if you had a copy that I could look at."

"I'm sorry, no. But I might be able to tell you . . . what were you looking for?"

"To see what was said about the Damerel's treasure being buried at Burntside Hall."

"Nobody in the dale believes that story."

"No, but there might have been some more detail. . .and the detail might be right, even though the main part of the story was wrong."

Micklefield smiled. "That's an interesting suggestion. Unfortunately it has been thought of before, and it doesn't happen to be accurate. Clough mentions the dairy. . . which is a ruin now, incidentally, not even a picturesque one."

"Then don't you think the dairy at Brass Castle—?" He broke off and added ruefully, "No, you said you'd taken up the floor of one of the farm buildings, didn't you? I suppose that was what you meant."

"I'm afraid it was," said the professor apologetically. "We took up the flags, and we dug it over methodically. There was nothing whatever there."

Antony picked up his coffee cup. "Wasn't that rather a big job?"

"Not so very."

"But the dairy. . .oh, I see what you mean. The present dairy isn't the original one."

"Early eighteenth century, as are the other farm buildings. The original dairy is now used as a larder, or was when Dodgson was there."

"The little room behind the kitchen, built right into the side of the hill?"

"That's right. Brass Castle was originally quite a small house, you know, with the mistal and loft adjoining. Those have now been made into the kitchen and two extra bedrooms, I believe."

"Yes, Bill told me. The kitchen floor still slopes from back to front; I expect they forgot to level it when they made the change." He drank some coffee and smiled at the professor. "If I'm going to have any bright ideas about where the treasure is hidden, I can see I'm going to have to think again."

"I'm sorry to disappoint you."

"I wouldn't say I was disappointed, exactly. I just find the story you told me rather a fascinating one." He thought of Jenny, and asked the question she had raised. "Do the newspapers ever refer to it? I imagine it would always be good for a paragraph... something to fill up space."

Micklefield looked at him in silence for a moment, and when he spoke he sounded almost disconcerted. "It's odd that you should ask that. There was a mention in the *Ellerdale Advertiser* just before Christmas by a man who writes for them regularly, Edward Ryder. He does an article every week on matters of local interest; it certainly isn't the first time he's referred to the lost treasure of the Damerels, by any means."

"Did he mention Brass Castle?"

"So far as I recollect, no." He paused again, looking at Antony quizzically. "I wish I knew how your mind was working, Mr. Maitland."

"I don't think it's so much working as scurrying about aimlessly," Antony admitted. "The thing is, I'm wondering if somebody who has only heard the story recently isn't interested, too." He proceeded to outline his theory, as he had done to Bill and Jenny the evening before.

Professor Micklefield was politer than Bill had been, but just as skeptical, and when the subject had been mulled over thoroughly he changed it by asking, "Have you seen yesterday's *Advertiser*?"

"Bill brought a copy home, I think. I haven't looked at it yet."

"Ryder was writing about Thorburndale again... the rumor I told you about, that a coven is meeting again in How Gill."

"What did he say?"

"Just that, in a suitably amused style."

"Nothing about Bess?" said Antony with sudden anxiety.

"He could hardly mention her by name."

"I don't like it, though. It means the story is fairly

widespread." He hesitated a moment, and then asked bluntly, "Do you believe it, sir?"

"Hardly," said Micklefield, a little taken aback.

"Something must have started them off," said Antony, dissatisfied.

"The coincidence of Bess Foster's name—"

"Yes, I suppose so." Anyway, it was of no use to labor the point. They went on to talk of other things, and Antony didn't leave until the coffeepot was empty. "Do you mind if I stroll around and take a look at the farm?" he asked as the professor escorted him to the door.

"Why, of course not. I would have suggested it if I had thought you'd be interested. Would you like me to come?"

"I don't want to disturb you any more than I have already."

"Well, Dodgson is sure to be about the farmyard; he will show you anything you want to see."

That, as it happened, was just what Antony wanted.

He found Seth Dodgson helping to unload some sacks of feeding stuff from a lorry that was backed in at the farmyard gate. The driver was a little man, but he was moving the heavy sacks as effortlessly as Dodgson was, so that Antony became simultaneously more aware of the pain in his shoulder and conscious of a distinct pang of envy. The job was nearly finished, however; he didn't have long to wait. Dodgson watched until the lorry had cleared the gateway without scratching either of the posts, and then crossed the yard to where Antony was standing.

"Sorry to keep you, Mr. Maitland. Is there owt I can do for you?"

"I've just left Professor Micklefield. He said you'd show me around."

"Glad to." He was a much more enthusiastic

guide than Cyril Thornton, and the tour took much longer. There were the pigs to see, the breeding sows and the ones that were being fattened for bacon; the small dairy herd, and the young bull that Norman coveted; the hens—light Sussex—and the handsome cockerel. The buildings were more extensive than those at Brass Castle, more orderly than those at Stavethorpe Hall. Antony admired everything, quite genuinely, as it happened, and Seth Dodgson seemed in a mellow mood when they finally halted outside the barn door.

"That's about t'lot," he said in a satisfied tone. "Nice to find you so interested, Mr. Maitland, and you from London."

"It makes a nice change."

Dodgson was nothing, if not direct. "How's Mr. Cleveland getting on, then?"

"Very well, so far as I can judge," said Antony deprecatingly. And then, with no change of tone, "There seems to be a story going around that he's thinking of leaving Brass Castle."

"Aye, so I've heard."

"Just what did you hear, Mr. Dodgson?"

"That he'd be selling up."

"It isn't true."

"It's not easy making a go of things without much capital these days," said Dodgson, unconvinced.

"I daresay it isn't. But be that as it may," said Antony, stretching the truth a little, "he told me yesterday that he was doing much better than he expected."

"It's early days yet."

"Precisely," said Antony, echoing for a moment unconsciously Sir Nicholas Harding's manner...a trick that Jenny sometimes complained of. "But you could tell anybody, couldn't you—anybody who was interested—that there is no question whatever...I expect you understand what I mean."

"I think I do, Mr. Maitland." If Dodgson felt a rebuke to be implicit in Antony's words he gave no sign of it, but smiled at him with his cheerfulness unimpaired. "If anybody should ask me...it isn't likely, mind."

He'd done what he could to put the record straight, and done it, he hoped, without arousing too much resentment. "I didn't know until Professor Micklefield told me," said Antony, beginning to walk toward the gate, "that you once lived at Brass Castle yourself."

"For nigh on fifteen years. There weren't so much land then. Ran it single-handed, I did...well, except for t'wife, you know."

"It's a nice place."

"It is that."

"The professor was telling me, too, about the treasure hunt."

Dodgson laughed. "A lot of nonsense," he said. "Still, that was when I first got to know t'professor, so I suppose you can say it did me a bit of good."

"You didn't think there might be anything in the story?"

"Not likely."

"Yet I've been told it's commonly held to be true."

"Some folk would believe anything," said Seth scornfully. But he seemed to have tired of the subject. "Miss Foster...Bess Foster," he said, with a sidelong look at Antony. "How is she bearing up?"

"It's a sad time for her." The triteness of the words was as good a disguise as any for the sudden distaste he felt.

"So it was arsenic Mrs. Thornton had."

"It seems so."

"I didn't see you at inquest, Mr. Maitland."

"I was standing at the back. I didn't see you, for that matter. Were you there?"

"A mark of respect, like," said Dodgson, again with that sidelong look that seemed to be appraising his companion's mood. "Being as she was a neighbor and all. I've heard it said that police was at Brass Castle this past week, with a question or two for t'lass."

"They could hardly have done other than take her evidence." He had sought this meeting deliberately, and one of his objects he had, perhaps, achieved, but now he was suddenly anxious to be gone.

"Not under t'circumstances," said Dodgson, with what sounded like a sinister emphasis on the phrase. "They'd wonder—well, it wouldn't be human nature not to wonder, would it, Mr. Maitland—why she left her home."

He could answer that quite simply with the truth; he could follow his instinct and snub Dodgson; but either way might open the door to further gossip. "I don't think it's really a very difficult question to answer," he said noncommittally. Dodgson could make what he liked out of that. They had been standing in the gateway while they talked, but now he went out onto Brown's Hill. When he turned to say goodbye and saw the other man's eyes bright with interest, he wondered if it would have been better to say nothing at all.

As he climbed toward High Lane a truck passed him, coming from the direction of Stavethorpe Edge. This time he took more notice of it, and even jotted down the number on an envelope he found in his pocket, after it had gone past. It might, or might not, be the one he had seen before; in any event it was likely, he thought, to be about its perfectly lawful occasions. All the same he wondered, as he went on his way, whether it was go-

ing to Ferrenscross Farm, or down the long hill into
Winterscale.

II

WHEN ANTONY GOT BACK to Brass Castle, Bill, who
was scratching Grunter's back in the sunshine
while her litter made their first tentative approach
to a bowl of weaner pellets, reported that the men
had been to repair the telephone line, and that five
minutes after it was in order again Margot Damerel
had called to ask them all to lunch the following
day. "I cried off," he said. "There's plenty to do
here, even if it is a Sunday, and Norman is going
over to Priest Monkton. I wouldn't wonder if he's
courting. But it will make a nice change for you and
Jenny."

"We don't really need a nice change, you know.
We're perfectly happy here."

"That's what Jenny said. I told her she was en-
titled to a day off; she's been working pretty hard."

"Which is more than can be said for me," said Antony gloomily. "As far as concentration goes, I seem
to have struck a bad patch."

"You've had plenty to distract you. Anyway, I
thought you'd like to meet the Damerels, in view of
the interest you're taking in local affairs."

"I shall, of course." His interest went deeper
than he would have been willing to admit. "Is Bess
going?"

"She wasn't mentioned. I don't think they can
know she's staying here."

"Probably not," Antony agreed, though privately
he thought it was most unlikely that there was anyone in the dale that didn't know it.

"Anyway, I expect she'll want to go home to
Stavethorpe Hall again," said Bill, sounding discon-
solate.

"She seems to have a strong sense of duty." That was as far as he could go toward reassurance. Perhaps it was too far. He went on to tell Bill about his talk with Professor Micklefield, but for some reason he did not mention that he had also seen Seth Dodgson. And he didn't mention the article in the *Advertiser* . . . time enough for that if Bill happened to read it. For the first time in his life he didn't feel completely at ease with his friend.

## 10

THEY WERE HAVING TEA, the three of them, when the police arrived. Bess was still at Stavethorpe Hall. Bill went to the door, and looked and sounded bewildered when he found Inspector Walton and Sergeant Holroyd on the doorstep. "I'm afraid Miss Foster isn't here at the moment," he said.

Walton was peering past him into the living room. "As a matter of fact, it was Mr. Maitland we wanted to see. And you might be able to help us, too, Mr. Cleveland, for all I know."

"I don't see how." But he stood back from the doorway. "You'd better come in, both of you, and have some tea."

"That's a kind thought," said the inspector. Sergeant Holroyd followed him into the room. Bill introduced them quickly to Jenny, forgetting the brief encounter the day before in Great Allerton, and fetched two extra cups from the sideboard. Jenny refilled the heavy teapot from the kettle on the hearth, and dealt in silence with the visitors' needs.

Antony watched in silence, too, until both the policemen were comfortably settled, and then, when neither of them showed any immediate disposition to state their business, prompted gently, "Well, Inspector?"

Walton eyed the plate Bill was proffering, as though the slices of homemade tea cake posed some insuperable problem of selection. "Well, Mr. Maitland," he replied, annoyingly.

"Are you still investigating Mrs. Thornton's death?"

"We are." He made his choice, and nodded his thanks to Bill, and turned his eyes and his attention to Antony.

"But that can't be—can it—why you want to talk to me."

"You're quite right, of course."

Bill said, "What on earth—?"

Jenny said anxiously, "Something else has happened." Antony looked from Walton to Holroyd, and then back at the inspector again.

"You'd better tell us," he suggested.

"Yes, of course." He didn't seem in any hurry to proceed, however, but finished his tea cake first, and put down his plate. "A man has been murdered," he said deliberately.

Bill's response had a sharpness he had not, perhaps, intended. "Who?" he asked.

"A neighbor of yours, Seth Dodgson." And, anticipating the next question, "At some time shortly after noon today."

"I was with him this morning," said Antony. Jenny picked up her teacup, and it rattled against the saucer as though her hand wasn't quite steady. Bill said nothing, but eyed the detective frowningly.

"So I understand," said Walton, nodding. "At what time did you leave him, Mr. Maitland?"

"At...oh, about ten to twelve, I should think. Do you remember what time I got in, Bill?"

"Half an hour before dinnertime, more or less," said Bill, still looking puzzled. "Who killed Seth, Inspector? And why?"

"I'm afraid I can't answer either of those questions, Mr. Cleveland."

"You mean you don't know."

"Not yet. That's why I'm hoping Mr. Maitland may be able to help me."

"Was I the last person to see him alive?" Antony asked, and Walton nodded again. "How was he killed?"

He expected that query would earn him a snub, but the detective seemed in an unexpectedly mellow mood. He started to speak, glanced at Jenny, and rather obviously toned down what he had been about to say. "He was struck repeated blows about the head with some blunt instrument."

Bill gave a crack of laughter, and sobered again immediately. "I didn't think anybody ever really said that," he explained apologetically. "Don't you know what was used?"

"We haven't found the weapon."

"A tire lever, or something like that would have done the trick," said Holroyd, who had quietly demolished the tea cake and turned his attention to a plate of gingerbread that Mrs. Dibb had produced regretfully in place of the parkin for which she could no longer get the ingredients. His deep voice and his sudden entry into the conversation startled them all, and Jenny spilled some of her tea.

"I think perhaps I can help you, Inspector," said Antony slowly, and began to feel in his pocket until he found the tattered envelope he had scribbled on that morning. "There was a cattle truck coming down Brown's Hill as I left Ferrenscross. I made a note of the number."

Walton took the envelope, studied what was written there for a moment, and then handed it to his subordinate. "Wasn't that rather an odd thing to do?"

"I don't think so. Constable Lister asked me if I'd seen any signs of black-market activity in the course of my walks."

"And you thought this truck—?"

"Not really. It might have interested him, that's all. Or not, as the case might be."

"I see," said Walton, borrowing one of Antony's favorite phrases and investing it with a rather sinister quality. "This would be at about ten minutes to twelve, you say?"

"If I'm right about the time." He was beginning to grow restless, though he recognized the reasonableness of Walton's questions. "I left Seth Dodgson at the gate to the farmyard, and was about halfway up the hill when the truck passed me."

"Going toward Ferrenscross?"

"I thought I made that plain."

"Did it stop there?"

"I was around the corner. I couldn't see."

"You might have heard."

"I didn't notice, I'm afraid."

"Can you describe—?"

"Just an ordinary cattle truck," said Antony irritably. "I think I've seen it before, but I'm not sure about that. It was painted red originally, but it's pretty shabby now. And the name on the cab door had been painted out."

"Thank you, Mr. Maitland. To go back a little, will you tell me about your visit to Ferrenscross this morning?"

"I really went to see Professor Micklefield."

"So I understand."

"That can't interest you."

"At the present stage of the investigation, everything interests me."

"Oh," said Antony, rather blankly, and thought about that for a moment. Walton maintained his air of rather passive interest, but at the same time succeeded very well in conveying the impression that he was willing to wait all day, if need be. "I know the time I left here, as it happens, half-past ten. And the walk takes twenty minutes, more or less. Professor Micklefield gave me coffee—"

"Had you any particular purpose in visiting him?"

"He's by way of being an expert on the history of this corner of Yorkshire. I wanted to ask him about a book I got out of the library that had some pages missing . . . whether he could fill in the missing information or not."

"And could he?" That was Holroyd again; he had finished the gingerbread by now, and seemed for the first time to be taking a genuine interest in what was going on.

"Yes," said Antony rather shortly. "After that we talked about the weather and the government . . . with particular reference to the Ministry of Agriculture and Fisheries."

"Was that all?"

"All I remember."

"Yet there are more immediate matters of interest in Thorburndale at the moment. The inquiry into black-market activities, for instance . . . Mrs. Thornton's death—"

"If I wanted to gossip, I don't think Professor Micklefield would be the partner I'd choose," said Antony, as repressively as his uncle might have done.

"I can understand that," Walton told him, as amiable as ever. "Was nothing said about Seth Dodgson, then?"

"Nothing. Except that, as I was leaving, I said I'd like to look at the farm, and the professor said I'd find Dodgson somewhere around the place and he would show me."

"And did you?"

"Find him? I already told you that."

"So you did. Well, now, Mr. Maitland, what can you tell us about that?"

"I suppose you mean was there anything unusual in his m-manner?" (Jenny and Bill both glanced at him uneasily; the slight stammer meant he was losing his temper, and it didn't seem that any good could come out of that.) "I only saw him once b-before, you know. He seemed just the s-same."

"And how was that?"

"Well...cheerful." He had brought his voice fairly well under control now. "Not anxious in any way."

"What did you talk about?"

"He was showing me around the farm; our conversation arose from that. I was interested, and he bore with my ignorance very well."

"Nothing else?"

"No." For the first time he sounded hesitant, and Walton took him up quickly.

"You seem in some doubt about that."

"Not really." (He couldn't say, "We talked about Bill's financial position," or "He had some pointed remarks to make about Bess Foster.") "He used to live at Brass Castle," he added more confidently. "He was talking about that."

"And when you left him...no signs of anxiety, you say."

"None at all. He came to the gate with me...the gate of the farmyard, that is. It was open, and he closed it, and stood leaning his elbows on it until I turned away."

"Waiting for somebody, perhaps."

"I couldn't say."

"No, of course. Well, you've been very patient with me, Mr. Maitland," said Inspector Walton politely, if inaccurately, and came to his feet as he spoke.

"Have I?" He grinned suddenly, seeing the humor of that. "Then perhaps you'll tell me something."

"What do you want to know?"

"Had this—Seth Dodgson's death—something to do with the black market?"

"I know nothing more than I've told you, Mr. Maitland. I'm not in a position to speculate." He let

that sink in for a moment, and then turned to Bill.
"Is it any use asking you, Mr. Cleveland, if you saw
anything that might be of interest to us?"

"Not a thing; I'm sorry."

"Or you, Mrs. Maitland?"

"No, nothing." She meant to leave it there but
added a moment later, lured perhaps by the inspector's bait of silence. "We're well insulated from the
road here, you know."

"Yes, I know," said Walton, a shade regretfully.
"All the same, I'd like to have a word with Norman
Dibb and his mother, if I may. There's always a
chance—"

"Yes, of course." Bill went toward the door
behind the staircase that led to the kitchen
quarters. Walton thanked Jenny for the tea, and
made his farewells, and took Sergeant Holroyd
away with him.

"There's a smooth character for you," said Antony bitterly as Bill shut the door and came back to
the fire again. Jenny glanced at him, and picked up
the teapot and weighed it in her hand. "No, I don't
want any more, thank you, love. What do you make
of that?"

"I don't like it," said Jenny decidedly. "It makes
me realize how easily Bill might have been killed,
too."

"Crime wave in Thorburndale," said Bill, making
light of it, but Antony took him up swiftly.

"Not very likely, is it?"

"Two unrelated murders. No, I suppose it isn't.
But—"

"But Mrs. Thornton and Mr. Dodgson couldn't
have anything to do with one another," Jenny objected.

"Couldn't they? Say Seth poisoned her—no, I
don't know why—and Thornton murdered him in
revenge." He looked from Jenny to Bill, and then

said more soberly, "Not funny...I know. What will Mrs. Dodgson do now?"

"Mrs. Dibb may know. I've an idea there's a daughter in Great Allerton. Meanwhile, I expect Norman will be willing to give them a hand at Ferrenscross until the professor can make some other arrangement. We can manage here, can't we, Jenny?"

"Yes, of course."

"I'll ask him, then, as soon as the police have gone. After that we'd better do the feeding, and I'll go and fetch Bess. If there's a murderer about—"

"Whoever killed Dodgson isn't likely to be hanging around."

"All the same—" said Bill stubbornly. It was obvious that he meant to have his own way.

II

THEY WERE BIDDEN FOR LUNCH at Dallow Park at one o'clock the next day, rather later than the usual Thorburndale dinner hour, so they set off just before half-past twelve by the most direct route across the packhorse bridge and up the path through the woods on the other side. Jenny had been rather quiet that morning...no cause for surprise, but he felt, without being told, that she was out of spirits. "The thing is, you've been too much with Bess," he said, as though they had been discussing the subject.

"What on earth do you mean?"

"You can't say she's been the most cheerful of companions."

"Poor girl, no." It was true, though. Her mood had brightened now that they had left Brass Castle. It was only with her next words that the idea came to him, annoyingly, that perhaps his own restlessness had been responsible.... "I've hardly seen Bess for the last two days," she reminded him.

"Don't be so literal minded, Jenny," he adjured her crossly. "You should have married Bill."

"I should, shouldn't I?" she agreed readily.

She was surprised when he said, his tone suddenly urgent, "Why didn't you?" Her laughter died and she looked at him blankly. "You could have done, couldn't you?" he insisted.

"I. . .I suppose—"

"Then why. . .oh, I know." He answered his own question savagely. "Can you imagine what it does to me, Jenny, to know. . .to know—"

"To know what, Antony?"

"What I've done to you. What I'm still doing to you, every day of our lives."

She didn't answer immediately, not until the silence was taut between them. Then she said quietly, "Are you still thinking about the baby?"

"Aren't you?"

"Sometimes." She would have lied readily enough, only she knew he wouldn't believe her. "It meant very little to me once I knew you were safe," she added with careful honesty, and thought it was often even more difficult to tell the truth.

"The fact remains that you can't have another."

"You can't blame yourself for that."

"Can't I?" he wondered, and added, bitterly, "Circumstances make an admirable alibi, don't they?"

Perhaps if she had asked him then, what happened to you during the three months I thought you were dead, he might have told her, though more likely he would have retreated into silence, leaving the question to lie forever unanswered between them. She never knew what instinct it was that prevented her. They had reached the bottom of the track now, and he had stopped halfway across the bridge to watch the sunlight dappling the water. He said, not looking at her, "If you weren't here, Jenny—"

"But I am here."

"Yes." He put out a hand and pulled her close to him, but he was still staring down at the Thorburn, dancing over the stones below. "If I could tell you what that means to me, love, it might seem more worthwhile to you, putting up with my moods."

"Antony, you know—" But he went straight on, disregarding the interruption.

"You're always so...always the same, Jenny. That's what I was trying to say to you. And I seem to be the only person who can upset that...that serenity."

"If that's true, it's because you're the only one I care about."

He turned his head then to look at her directly, and after a moment said in a shaken voice, "You really mean that, don't you?"

"Yes." She hesitated, and then, becoming uneasy under his fixed regard, said more lightly, "I'm afraid you'll have to put up with me, Antony. I think Bill's in love with Bess, so it's no use counting on him to take me off your hands."

For a moment his hand tightened on her own. Then he said, with something that was almost a groan, "Oh, Lord, yes, I think so, too." And Jenny had an instant of pure amusement, because she knew what he meant, but she might so easily have pretended to take it the wrong way.

Instead she asked, "Don't you think it's a good thing?"

"I wish to God I knew."

"I thought you liked Bess." It wasn't long since he had asked her that same question, but she saw no incongruity in it now.

"That has nothing to do with it. Don't you realize—it was you who made me aware of it first—she's more than half in love with Cyril Thornton?"

"I know I said...but I don't think I really believed it."

"Well, think about it now."

"But he's so old...Mr. Thornton, I mean."

"Fortyish, wouldn't you say?"

"Too old for Bess. And anyway...it's horrible. As if all the things that are being said about them were true."

"Now you're exaggerating. All I'm worried about is that Bill may get hurt."

"Yes, of course. But do you suppose...do you think Mr. Thornton—?"

"I don't think he was in love with his wife."

Jenny digested this for a moment in silence. "It doesn't follow that he's fond of Bess."

"No." He released her hand, which he had been holding all this time. "Did you see Ryder's 'Country Notes' in the *Advertiser*?"

"About the witches...yes. It didn't say anything that mattered."

"Did Bill see it, do you know?"

"He hasn't mentioned it. I don't think he can have done."

"That's good." He wasn't quite sure why he felt it was important. "We'd better be getting on if we don't want to be late. Have I taken your appetite away?"

"I shouldn't think so." Jenny took a deep breath and followed him off the bridge onto the south bank of the river. "Don't you think," she said hopefully, "Bess might get over it? If she is in love with Mr. Thornton, I mean."

"I shouldn't worry too much about it, love, until we know if my first premise is right."

"No." She sounded doubtful. "Things have changed, haven't they, since Mrs. Thornton died?"

"Not really. It's just that we've got to know a bit more about the people who live here."

"I suppose there are always things hidden." (Just as nobody looking at you would realize, Antony, that you can't bear to be reminded...or perhaps, looking at me, would know how painful it is to watch you struggling....) "Things like this just stir them up." They had reached the edge of the trees now and she paused an instant, unwilling to leave the sunlight. "What do you suppose Uncle Nick will think if we stay here much longer?"

He was startled by the echo of his own thought. "I don't know. I almost wish—"

"That he'd order us home?"

"I wouldn't go."

"I see."

"I daresay you do. Don't worry, Jenny."

"No," she agreed with a docility he immediately suspected. But before he could say anything more she turned the subject, saying reflectively, "Do you really think Mr. Damerel's housekeeper might have made a mistake?"

"I don't suppose for a moment she made only one jar of gooseberry jam. Someone else would have died, or at least been ill, in the meantime."

"But that means—"

"It could have been poisoned anytime after it was opened. Plenty of people had the opportunity to do so, according to what Thornton told us."

"But Mrs. Thornton had been having bilious attacks before that...ever since May."

"That could have given the poisoner the idea."

"How gruesome," said Jenny, and gave an elaborate shudder. "Do you think...wouldn't it be a good idea, Antony, if we talked about something else?"

"Who started the subject, I should like to know?"

"Did I? Well, now I'm changing it. I had a thought the other evening when you were talking about the treasure hunters."

"I don't know that that's much of an improvement," he said gloomily.

"Oh, it is. We don't even know for sure that anybody is looking for treasure, and if they are, they're strangers."

Privately he thought that wasn't much of a recommendation. "All right, then," he said. "What was your thought?"

"Well, you were talking about *them*, and do you know who you seemed to be describing? The black-market people."

"That occurred to you, too, did it? I'm beginning to think there might be something in the theory."

"At least, if they're frequenting Thorburndale they might easily have heard about the treasure. And if they're making money out of black-market operations they can't be too scrupulous."

"There's another point you haven't mentioned. We know, because Constable Lister told us, that they're predisposed to violence."

"He told Bill, and Bill told us."

"You're being literal again, but it comes to the same thing. They wouldn't have thought twice about hitting Bill over the head. And now there's what happened to Seth Dodgson."

"Do you suppose that was something to do with the black market?"

"It seems likely. He could have had quite a nice little racket going on the side without the professor knowing anything about it."

"Then why should they kill him?"

"I don't know. He was the source of most of the local rumors, so far as I can tell. Someone might have wanted to shut his mouth." He paused as they came out into the sunlight again with Dallow Park in full view, and then added in a thoughtful tone, "It makes you wonder what will happen next."

There should have been nothing in the words to

make her feel that he needed reassurance, but she said rather quickly, "Nothing, perhaps."

"I wouldn't count on that, if I were you."

"No...well...we shall have to wait and see, that's all." She stopped again, this time looking up at the building they were approaching. "Mr. Damerel was right. It *is* ugly, isn't it?"

"He didn't say it was ugly, though I agree with you it is. He said it was uncomfortable."

"I wonder why," said Jenny, walking on. But it became obvious later, when Margot Damerel, with a sort of pride in its inconveniences, showed them the house.

Dallow Park was said to be of Tudor architecture, though standing on the site of a much earlier house, but it had very little in common with any place, of any period, that they had ever seen. It was four stories in height and had originally had four rooms to each story, though these had been subdivided now on the upper floors to provide corridors and bathrooms, and ensure the occupants a little privacy, at least when they went to bed. Downstairs the rooms still led one to another, and as the kitchen was on the ground floor and the dining room (not directly above it) one floor up, and as the only means of access from one story to the next was a winding stair in a projecting turret at the rear of the house, the point that it might have been more handily arranged hardly needed laboring. When the tour was finished they went into the library, a big, square box of a room, but comfortably furnished, and with a roaring fire of proper logs..."proper" as opposed to the scrap wood that Bill was burning.

Antony thought that Margot Damerel was about his own age, Jenny that she was "much older," though this decision was based on a rather self-confident manner, and she had to admit that Margot didn't look it. She was very like her father—

a strong face, handsome perhaps, certainly not beautiful. But she was slim and elegant—no mean achievement in postwar England—so that Jenny felt more than usually conscious of her darned stockings and shabby coat. Patrick, probably younger than his sister, had his father's build and not much else. Fair hair, blue eyes, an indeterminate air about him. He had done his stint, he said, in the air force, ground crew, and now was at an agricultural college in Beverley.

"Dad was furious with your friend Cleveland," he said; he was handing around sherry as he spoke, and didn't sound as though he meant to be taken seriously. "He wanted Brass Castle, you know."

"So Bill told me."

"My emotions stopped short of fury, in spite of what Patrick says," said Wilfred Damerel. He sounded casual and amused, but Antony had the sudden feeling that, on this subject at least, the son might have spoken more truly than he knew.

He said, "I'm glad of that," and matched the older man's casual tone, but he was uneasy, as always when an acquaintanceship was in the "discovery" stage, because sooner or later there would be questions. But this time later, rather than sooner. There was first the topic of Seth Dodgson's death to explore.

Damerel had heard of it from one of the farmhands, who in turn had been told of it after chapel in Winterscale. But Antony's visit to Ferrenscross wasn't mentioned, so presumably that wasn't common knowledge yet. "I hope you don't think life in Thorburndale is always as eventful as this," said Wilfred, with a quizzical look.

"Mrs. Dibb says troubles never come singly," Jenny told him.

"She went further than that," Antony put in. "She said they always come in threes."

"Then I sincerely hope she's wrong." Damerel sounded more startled than the pronouncement seemed to warrant. "Did you know Dodgson at all?"

"Not to say know him. I'd met him a couple of times."

"He was a gossip."

"So I gathered."

"But harmless enough, I should have thought."

"I wonder," said Margot. She sounded provocative, but neither her father nor brother seemed inclined to take up the speculation. Instead, Wilfred Damerel turned to Antony, and gave the conversation—to his discomfort—rather an obvious jerk in another direction.

"You're reading law, aren't you?" he asked. "Margot was in the W.A.A.F., but now she's secretary to a lawyer in Leeds, so you have that much in common. But what was your line during the war?"

"Army, sir. A staff job in London." Which was one of those half-truths that are often more misleading than a direct lie. He wasn't looking at Jenny, but he heard her give a little sigh, as though with relief that he had given, for once, a reasonable-sounding answer to what was, after all, a purely routine inquiry. "As for Jenny, she drove an ambulance."

"Were you in London, too? I didn't think you were old enough—"

"I wasn't, at first. I was at home in the country and we had evacuees...dozens of them," said Jenny, exaggerating cheerfully now that the danger point was passed. "Then when I was seventeen I went on a course the ambulance service gave, and after that...yes, I was in London. We were married in 1943."

At least that ought to clear the way for some more

innocuous subject. There was a little silence, not
awkward, and then Margot said, "Dad tells me
you're interested in local history."

It was more query than statement, and it seemed
to be divided equally between them. "Buried
treasure in particular," Antony said, and sipped his
sherry, which was pleasantly dry.

"So I heard," said Wilfred. He sounded diverted.

After nearly three weeks in Thorburndale he
shouldn't be surprised any longer how news got
about, but he couldn't help asking, "Who told
you?"

"Seth Dodgson."

"Did he though?" Well, there was nothing to be
surprised at in that. "Professor Micklefield was
very helpful in my researches."

"I'm sure he was." There was a distinct flavor of
irony about Damerel's agreement. "He is not, however, quite so well informed on that particular point
as he believes."

"I thought—"

"I daresay you did. What, for instance, did he tell
you about the family at Brass Castle at the time of
the Civil War?"

"Nothing much . . . their names, when they were
born. Just what could be gathered from the parish
records at Winterscale." He paused, looking back
on the two conversations he had had with the professor. "It left me wondering which of them was
the servant the legend mentions." Damerel was
smiling now. "Is there more to it than that?"

"A good deal more. Micklefield thinks he has
made a study of the circumstances, but he has not—
shall we say—my resources."

"Surely he applied to you—"

"Oh, he did. He came to me early in the year that
ridiculous treasure hunt was held. He didn't need
my permission, of course, but I told him quite plain-

ly it was a fool's errand. If he wouldn't listen to advice, that wasn't my concern. But, that being so, it hardly seemed worthwhile to give him the additional information that came later to my disposal.''

''You don't like him,'' said Jenny, with one of the flashes of shrewdness that always took Antony by surprise. Not that she had them, but that she gave them voice.

And Damerel threw back his head and laughed, and then said amiably, ''How did you guess?''

Jenny laughed, too. ''It wasn't difficult. But he—both of them—seemed awfully nice to me.''

''Then we must agree to differ.''

''Will you tell us—?''

''What, my dear?''

''I don't want to ask anything you'd prefer not to answer, but we did get rather fascinated—'' She didn't try to finish that, but glanced at Antony as though for support. But Antony was watching Wilfred Damerel's face, and thinking again that Margot was very like him, and that the father, at least, had a thread of malice in his nature that had not been apparent at their first meeting. All the same, he hoped he would tell them. . . but Jenny's tongue, he felt, would prove the more persuasive.

He was surprised when Damerel said, without further ado, and with an expansive gesture, ''My dear child, there's no secret about it. I have some of the volumes of Hugh Ambler's journal.''

''Hugh? I don't quite remember—'' said Jenny, wrinkling her forehead.

''The son of the Ambler who lived at Brass Castle,'' Antony prompted her. ''Was he the servant, sir?''

''The one who took charge of the treasure, yes, that much seems clear, though Margaret Ambler—the younger Margaret—was also in service with my family. The foresters were traditionally the king's men, as we were.''

"Wasn't there another sister?"

"Helen. She was bedridden . . . paralyzed. Some form of poliomyelitis, it sounds like, though of course it wouldn't have been diagnosed at that date."

"Was all that in the journal?"

"That and much more." It was obvious that he was enjoying their interest. "I would show you the original if it weren't lodged at my bank, but in any event you wouldn't be much the wiser. It isn't easy to decipher; in fact, I'm indebted to Father O'Malley in Great Allerton for making a transcript for me last year. He is interested in the period, but I doubt if I should have had the patience to do it myself."

"Hadn't it been done before?"

"Not to my knowledge. I don't suppose I was the first Damerel to read it, but certainly my father, and my grandfather, and probably several generations before them, knew nothing of its content. Or even of its existence. It—there were several volumes, as I told you—was lodged behind a set of very dull early nineteenth-century sermons that nobody in their right mind would think of taking down to read."

"But wasn't it rather extraordinary that a smallholder's son should have been so fluent with his pen?" He hadn't realized he had finished his sherry, but Patrick was refilling his glass, and he made a mental note not to drink this one so quickly. Wilfred Damerel was going on with his dissertation.

"The journal doesn't cover Hugh's boyhood, but I think I can tell you how it must have come about. The family chaplain was the only Catholic priest for miles around; a fairly open secret, it seems to have been, but a secret nevertheless in those dangerous times. If the Amblers still kept to the old faith, the children would most likely be sent to get their religious instruction from him, and if Hugh proved an apt pupil that might not have been all he learned. He grew up to serve young Edward d'Aumerle, and followed him to the war, becoming a trooper in Prince Rupert's horse. Unfortunately he hadn't the time—or perhaps not the inclination—to write up his journal during his period of active service, but he does record that they rode home together in June 1644.''

"That was just before Marston Moor, wasn't it?"

"It was. I'm inclined to think they must have had some mission... some message to deliver, perhaps. Hugh's notes strike me as evasive. He is more concerned to record that they met his sister—Meg, he calls her—when they were just about to part at the packhorse bridge. He thought she was in love with Edward, which he didn't consider seemly, but when he took her to task for it the next day he got a pert reply.''

"What did he expect?'' demanded Margot.

"That she would show him a little of the respect due to an older brother, perhaps,'' said Patrick, sitting down again, which made Antony wonder whether he had been mistaken about their respective ages. Margot laughed and relaxed. She had a habit of stretching like a cat. In fact, Jenny thought with a lack of charity that was unusual in her, there was something altogether feline about the other girl.

"Anyway,'' Margot said, "Meg got married only two months later, so perhaps she listened to his admonitions, after all.''

"Yes,'' Patrick agreed. "And he found something to moralize about in that, too.''

Wilfred Damerel had been listening to this exchange with his air of having some secret cause of amusement. "I think I can remember his exact words,'' he said now. And quoted, "'I have advised the said Simon that he beat her well, that certain sick fancies of her mind may thereby be cured.' "

Antony murmured, "Obviously a disciple of Saint Paul."

Jenny said, "Well!" and this time Wilfred laughed openly at her indignation. "I suppose she was really in love with Edward," she added, thoughtfully, "but I can't see that it would be the slightest use—"

Antony wasn't interested in Meg Ambler and her problems, but, for the moment, was single-mindedly following out the thread of his own ideas. "The really important thing is, what did the journal have to say about the treasure?"

"It gave an itemized list," said Wilfred. This time it was Margot who interrupted.

"That's why the journal is in the bank," she said. "To help prove ownership in case anything is ever found. The descriptions of some of the jewelry make your mouth water, though I suppose if you saw them the settings would be absolutely hideously old-fashioned."

"Besides that there were simply masses of gold plate," said Patrick. "That would be pretty valuable today."

"Not to mention the things that belonged to the church."

"But surely—" Antony broke off and started again. "Didn't he say *where* he'd hidden it?"

"That's the joke," Margot told him. "What he wrote must have been deliberately to deceive any unauthorized person who read the journal, because it wasn't true."

"What?"

Wilfred Damerel took up the story again, and again he was quoting, " 'and went therewith to my father's house.' Of course, it wasn't called Brass Castle then," he added. "That was the name the local people gave it, consequent upon the rumor of hidden wealth.''

''Then how can you be sure it's the same place?''

''You didn't let me finish. 'My father's house at Stavethorpe top.' The same description occurs in the manor rolls, against Richard Ambler's name, and later is added 'now commonly called Brass Castle,' which is pretty conclusive, I should say.''

''I see.''

''And to answer the question that I'm quite sure is hovering on the tip of your tongue, he goes on, 'By whose aid the same was secreted privily in the dairy.' He spells that d-a-i-r-e-y, but I don't think there's any doubt what he meant.''

''Tautology,'' said Margot, and Antony gave her a rather absentminded smile before he went back to the point at issue.

''Professor Micklefield says—''

''Precisely,'' said Wilfred Damerel, as though somehow he had scored a point. ''He and his minions took up the flags and dug up the floor beneath them.''

''Are you sure they went deep enough?''

''My information is that they went as deep as they could go... which wasn't very far, before they came to rock.''

''The translation—no, the transcription, you called it—of the journal hadn't been made then.''

''No. At that time I didn't even know the journal existed. Micklefield got his information from a book some fellow wrote—''

''Clough.''

''That's right. He'd got the story half right, half wrong. Or all wrong, as it turned out.''

''I wonder how that came about.''

''I don't know. But it would only need one dalesman who resented his questions to invent a story—''

"And they can be a bloody-minded lot," Patrick put in.

"Yes. I see," said Antony again. "And was that all Hugh Ambler had to say?"

"All about the treasure," said Margot, and exchanged a smile with her brother.

"What happened to him after that?"

"He survived Marston Moor and went into exile with Edward," said Wilfred Damerel. "He didn't stay with him, though; he went to Douai to train as a priest, and eventually came back after his ordination to live out his life in Thorburndale—he was one of the lucky ones—as family chaplain. Of necessity a secluded existence, but he seems to have been happy enough."

"Then if your people had wanted to dig up the treasure, there was nothing to stop them."

"Nothing except the hazards of the times they lived in."

"But later. . . you said, didn't you, that they were in favor with Charles II? Did Hugh die before the Restoration?"

"The journals stop in 1658, though they hadn't been kept seriously for some years before that. For lack of matter, I suppose. There's no record of his death in the family papers, or of where he was buried."

"But surely he told *somebody*—" Antony sounded exasperated, and Wilfred Damerel smiled at him.

"You can't feel more strongly about it than I do. The fact remains that the tradition in the family is that the treasure was never recovered."

"Not even in secret?"

"I don't think so. I believe—I may be wrong, but I firmly believe—that it would have been reflected in the family fortunes. Which have been at ebbtide since the penal times, I may say."

"Was that why you wanted to buy Brass Castle?"

asked Jenny, putting into words the very question Antony was hesitating over.

"For sentimental reasons? Yes, I suppose so. Patrick will need somewhere to try out his ideas when he leaves the agricultural college. But I'd no hope of succeeding at this late date where others have failed."

"I thought perhaps—" said Jenny. Damerel shook his head at her.

"You're a romantic, my dear. You and your husband."

Antony smiled at him. "Romantic or not," he said, not believing for an instant that there was any truth in the assertion, "I'd be glad if you'd tell me one thing."

"Anything within reason."

That was said lightly, but Antony thought there was a genuine note of caution. "When did Father O'Malley make this transcription of Hugh Ambler's journal?"

"It took him some time. He finished the work and handed the typescript over to me early last year . . . in February or March, I should say."

"Did you tell anyone?"

"It was hardly a secret."

"No, but . . . I wish you'd try to remember."

"Cyril and Hester Thornton. I thought they'd be interested, living in the dale. And I think I mentioned it to Undercliffe for the same reason."

"About the treasure?"

"That was the main point of interest."

"Father O'Malley kept a copy, I suppose."

"I suppose so. I wish I knew what you were getting at," he added, and now his tone was faintly querulous.

"Idle curiosity," said Antony vaguely, and glanced at Margot. "Somehow I got the impression that we hadn't quite finished with what Hugh Ambler had to say."

**11**

THIS TIME Margot didn't look at her brother, but she was smiling when she answered. "Father didn't tell you all that happened the day Hugh Ambler and Edward d'Aumerle rode home from the war."

"They met his sister, Meg, at the packhorse bridge."

"Before that."

"They met the witch, Bess Foster, as they rode through How Gill," said Patrick, getting up again to circulate with the decanter. There was no mistaking the fact that he spoke in malice. "Funny, isn't it, the way that name keeps on cropping up?"

"Would you say it was an uncommon one?"

"Not hereabouts, except that the more usual diminutives of Elizabeth would be Betty, nowadays, or Beth. But you know what the country folk are saying. Even the descriptions tally."

"I thought the whole seventeenth-century story about Bess Foster was nothing more than a rumor."

"I don't think you can class what Hugh Ambler wrote as a rumor."

"Not that I ever told anybody about *that* part of the journal," said Wilfred Damerel rather hurriedly, as though he sensed the visitors' distaste for the subject.

"Allowing for the fact that she was no longer young when he saw her—"

"He said she was dirty," Margot objected, holding out her glass to him. "And bent with age."

"That isn't to say she had always been like that."
Patrick was full of enthusiasm for his subject. "He
said she was tall for a woman, and had fair hair. . .
yes, I admit he said it straggled on her shoulders,
but so would yours if you lived in a hovel with no
modern conveniences. And he said when she
looked at him for a moment directly he saw that her
eyes were a deep, gentian blue. . .and you can't say
he was a poetic sort of chap, so she must have made
an impression on him. And he also said, in his rather
stuffy way, that it was obvious she had been handsome in her youth."

"All the same—" Antony broke off there, because any protest he made was likely to be too
forceful for politeness, and looked rather helplessly
at his host.

Damerel said, "Do you really think, Patrick—?"
but (to the surprise of both the Maitlands, as they
found when they compared notes afterward) the
remonstrance was far from forceful, and Patrick
disregarded it.

"You know what they're saying about Bess and
Cyril," he said relentlessly. "It makes a neat
parallel with the old story about Bess Foster and
Henry Robinson."

"Patrick—"

"Don't worry, father. As long as nobody believes
it. . .none of us, I mean. I don't, and I'm sure neither
Antony nor Jenny has any faith in witchcraft."

"The tale could be harmful," said Damerel, more
firmly, "without bringing such matters into it at
all."

"Well, as to that," said Margot, who had been
listening in silence, but with a distinctly cream-fed
look, "If somebody really poisoned the gooseberry
jam—"

Antony pounced on that. "But, did they?"

"The police seem to think so. They've taken the

whole batch away to send to Wakefield, but they won't find anything in it, of course. And if there *was* anything in Hester's jar, I'd rather it was put in at Stavethorpe than here.''

''But if it was an accident—'' Wilfred didn't try to finish the sentence.

Margot said scornfully, ''How could it have been? Let's face it, if Mrs. Forbes had made a mistake like that, we'd all be dead by now.''

''That's as good as to say. . .that's slander. Isn't it?'' Damerel appealed to Antony.

''Not until you draw some conclusion from the facts.''

''But we all know—''

''Verbally, not mentally. In any case,'' he added, not altogether displeased to be turning the tables, ''if the arsenic was added at Stavethorpe Hall, I understand that quite a number of people—yourself included, sir—would have had the opportunity to do so.''

Damerel burst out laughing. He addressed his son and daughter impartially, and sounded all at once more sure of himself. ''You see where your theoriz-ing is leading us. Don't you think we'd better leave the subject alone?''

''I thought perhaps Antony was interested in that, too,'' said Patrick innocently.

''Don't be silly, Pat, he can't say he is,'' said Mar-got. ''Bess Foster is staying at Brass Castle, isn't she?''

''For the present,'' Antony admitted grudgingly. His tone ought to have ended the subject, but Patrick was persistent.

''Why?'' he asked.

''Because she's heard the gossip,'' said Jenny, unable to contain herself any longer. ''What would you feel like if people were saying things like that about you?''

"But, my dear!" said Margot, opening her eyes very wide. "Nobody could be blamed for disliking Hester." Jenny was looking at her without much expression, and showed no signs of being mollified. "*Really*," Margot added, in a coaxing voice, "she had a worse temper than anybody I ever knew."

"And she was mean. She had the money, you know; more than Cyril, at any rate. I wouldn't say he's exactly a success as a farmer, would you, father? But Hester would look at every sixpence twice before she'd spend it."

Bill had said something like that when he was talking about the sale of the farm; so had Professor Micklefield, if he remembered rightly. Antony said slowly, because he didn't like the feeling of ill will toward Thornton and Bess, but still Patrick had been so far right . . . he *was* curious. "I don't think he really likes farming." And Wilfred Damerel came back into the conversation with an air of relief that perhaps the worst was over.

"That's an understatement."

"Then why—?"

"He came into it by inheritance. There have been Thorntons at Stavethorpe for the last two hundred years."

"Not long, by your standards."

"No, indeed. But most of our land is over toward Ellerdale, which is rather more fertile."

"So I've heard. I don't know Ellerdale at all yet."

"Perhaps Mr. Thornton will be able to retire now," said Jenny.

"On what Hester had to leave?" said Damerel. "Not a chance. A few thousands at the most . . . not a fortune."

At that point they were summoned to the luncheon table, and the talk turned to other matters, less controversial. Jenny and Antony didn't leave until nearly half-past three, and by then they were all pretty well in charity with one another. But neither of them could forget altogether what had been said about the Thorntons and Bess, and Jenny answered with rather vague politeness when Margot spoke of another meeting.

## II

THE SUN HAD GONE IN NOW, the sky was gray, and the air felt damp, though it wasn't actually raining. In spite of this they went home the long way around at Antony's suggestion, making the crossing at Winterscale and coming up Brown's Hill past Ferrenscross. Everything was quiet—there had been a sabbath calm around Winterscale, too—but there was a police car parked close to the farmyard wall, and when they looked through the gate they could see a bicycle they recognized as Norman's propped up outside the milking parlor. Jenny said, "Do you suppose they've found out something else?"

Antony replied, "I don't know," which seemed effectively to close the subject. But they were occupied with their own thoughts, and had both forgotten the question again by the time they reached High Lane.

They found Bill standing in the doorway of Grunter's sty, watching her take her evening meal and looking considerably more cheerful than he had when they left that morning. He came out when he saw them, and smiled at Jenny when she said, "I'll change quickly and give you a hand."

"It's all done. Did you have a good time?"

Jenny said rather primly, "It was very interesting to see Dallow Park," which was so unlike her that Bill looked inquiringly at Antony.

"Didn't you like the Damerels?" he asked bluntly. There was something about him, a sort of suppressed excitement, that puzzled Antony; but better, perhaps, not to ask what it was in aid of.

Jenny said, "Oh, yes," very offhand, and Antony added, "They were extremely hospitable, and gave us a very good lunch. And some more information about the people who used to live here at the time of the Civil War."

"Did they?" said Bill, not evincing much concern. And then, rather overdoing the casual air, "Bess is in the barn. Big Pussy has had her kittens."

"I thought Bess was at Stavethorpe."

"She came back after lunch. I didn't tell Mrs. Dibb," said Bill, suddenly expansive, but addressing a point in the air midway between them, and with an undeniably fatuous look, "because I wanted you to be the first to know. Bess has promised to marry me."

Jenny said, "I'm so glad!" and gave what could only be construed as a triumphant look at Antony.

Antony said more slowly, because it took a moment to adjust his mind to the fact that his main worry had, after all, been groundless, "Congratulations! You're a lucky man."

Bill was looking from one to the other of them now, pleased with himself and with the small sensation he had caused. "The thing is," he confided, "I couldn't bear to see her so depressed. I thought I shouldn't ask her while she was staying here, but as things turned out,—"

"What things?" said Antony, and Jenny glanced at him impatiently. But Bill was giving the question his serious consideration.

"She's worried, you see. About Hester's death. Well, naturally she is. And then to cap everything the police were at Stavethorpe this morning asking if anyone had seen anything that might have a bearing on Seth Dodgson's murder."

"What of it? They were here, too, yesterday." Antony seemed in an argumentative mood.

"Yes, but this was different. They wanted to know if Cyril had been out, if he had an alibi. Routine, they said. I suppose *you'd* say that was natural enough," said Bill a little resentfully, "but Bess didn't see it that way."

"All the same, it would be just routine. I bet they asked Mrs. Dibb and Norman about you."

"Then why didn't they—?"

"You told me yourself that Bob Clayton isn't too bright." Bill still looked dissatisfied. "The important thing is, had Thornton an alibi?"

"Yes. Bess says he spoke to Mrs. Clayton at the back door at a quarter to twelve...she had her eye on the clock because of getting the potatoes on to boil. And then he came in at half past, and she noticed the time again because she was just dishing up. And nobody could possibly get from Stavethorpe to Ferrenscross and back again in three quarters of an hour."

"Not on foot," said Antony provokingly.

"Bob would have known if either the car or the tractor had been out, or if anyone had borrowed his bicycle; he's bright enough for that, and they hadn't. And anyway," said Bill, clinching the matter, "you'd have been bound to meet him yourself in High Lane."

"So I would. Don't be in a huff, Bill. I'm only trying to put myself in Walton's place."

"Is that what it is?" Bill's tone was a little dry, but he was in a complacent mood, quite ready to forgive and forget. "But you can see—can't you—that Bess didn't like it. It brought back the other business...the other questions...too vividly."

"At any rate, you can congratulate yourself that you've done what you can to take her mind off things," Antony suggested, and Bill laughed.

"That's one way of putting it," he said. "Seriously, Antony, do you think we should have waited until all the mystery is cleared up?"

"If you mean about Mrs. Thornton's death, that may never happen," Antony pointed out.

Jenny said impulsively, "I don't believe in waiting," so that Antony's mind went back to their talk on the way to Dallow Park, and he thought, but did not say, look where it's got you. But Jenny, he knew, and was comforted by the knowledge, never said things she didn't mean.

"No, I realize that," said Bill. He might have been answering either or both of them. "But I don't much like the idea that we shall never know—" He broke off there and his face cleared. "Here's Bess," he announced.

Bess was coming toward them from the direction of the barn. She was smiling, and she came and tucked her hand under Bill's arm and looked up at him. "Have you told them?" she said.

So all the good wishes were said again. Bess was quietly glowing, and Antony thought, looking at her, she's just the wife for Bill, I'm glad I was wrong about her feeling for Thornton. Perhaps her subdued air, all this time, had been due not so much to what had happened as to the fear that Bill might not share her feelings.

They went in to tea and gave Mrs. Dibb the news, and she appeared (so far as anyone can ever tell with a Yorkshirewoman) to give the affair her blessing. It was a happier gathering around the fire in the living room than there had been for some time, and when they had exhausted the subject of plans—which didn't take long, because Bess seemed quite content with the fact of her engagement, and to have no desire for the moment to look into the future—Antony reverted to the subject of the treasure, which seemed as safe a theme as any, and told them what he had learned about the Ambler family that day at Dallow Park.

"Was it Father O'Malley you had those dealings with over a pig?" he asked in conclusion.

"It was." Bill seemed slightly more interested to-day, less inclined, at least, to make light of Antony's ideas. "But I don't suppose he can tell you any more than Damerel did."

"That isn't the idea. I want to know how many people he told about the transcription."

"I don't suppose he can remember."

"He might."

"Anyway, why—?"

"Because, if my theory is right, there had to be some reason for the treasure hunters to change their sphere of activity from Burntside Hall to here."

"You said that perhaps Seth Dodgson—"

"I know what I said. It was only an idea, and probably all wrong."

"Well, what do you want me to do?" Bill was skeptical but resigned.

"If you phone Father O'Malley now, you'll catch him before Benediction."

"That's all very well, but what do you want me to say to him?"

"Ask him . . . no, introduce me, and let me talk to him."

"He'll think we're both mad."

"Give him credit for a little Christian charity," Antony suggested.

"Oh, very well." Bill got up and went to the phone. It took a little time for Father O'Malley to be found, but presently he was able to speak to him, and a moment later he turned and handed the receiver over to Antony, who took it with a show of confidence. Jenny began quietly to stack the tea things together.

"I'm sorry to bother you, Father."

"Sure, and 'tis no bother at all."

That was all very well, but he still wasn't sure how to word his query. "I was talking to Mr. Damerel today," said Antony, feeling his way.

"And how does he be after finding himself?" Exaggerated, and a little distorted by the telephone, the rich brogue had an effect of parody.

Whether or not the question was a rhetorical one, Antony decided to ignore it. "He was telling me about Hugh Ambler's journal," he said.

"Was he now?"

"And about the transcription you made for him. I was wondering, Father, whom you told about it."

"And why ever would you be wanting to know a thing like that?"

"It's a bit difficult to explain." That was greeted with silence, so he had no choice but to press on. "Some queer things have been happening in Thorburndale."

"They have, indeed."

"I mean, I've got the idea that somebody is making a serious attempt to find the treasure."

Father O'Malley laughed. "You're interested in it yourself," he asserted. The brogue was much less pronounced now; perhaps it was something he assumed on occasion for his own amusement. But the statement required an answer.

"Not in the way I think you mean. But, as I say, I think somebody else is. And it might explain—"

"Two murders?"

"There's nothing to say they're connected in any way," said Antony, instinctively taking the opposing view.

"Perhaps not," said Father O'Malley judiciously. "And nothing to connect them, either, with the Damerel's treasure."

"As a matter of fact, I wasn't thinking of the murders. . . either of them. There have been some other odd things. . . . And it's amusing to think," he went on ingenuously, "that I might be standing on top of a fortune at this very moment."

This time the priest's laughter nearly deafened him, so that he had to hold the receiver away from his ear. "I think I'm beginning to see what you mean," said Father O'Malley.

(Probably he puts me down as a romantic, as Damerel did, or said he did.) "Some of it belonged to the church," said Antony casually.

"And devil a penny of it *we'd* be seeing," said Father O'Malley cheerfully. But his curiosity seemed to be satisfied one way or another. "What was it you were wanting to know, then?"

"Whether you talked to anybody about the journal."

"And if I did, you'll be telling the police to clap the handcuffs on him?"

"Hardly."

"Well, no matter." It was obvious now that he was enjoying himself. "I spoke of it to one person only. One of my parishioners, Edward Ryder."

"I've heard that name before."

"He writes a regular column for the *Ellerdale Advertiser*."

"That chap?"

"Yes. He's something of a historian, so I knew he would be interested."

"Do you think he might have written about the journal?"

"I'm sure he didn't. I read his article every week and, though he mentioned 'the lost treasure of the Damerels' not long ago, he made no reference to the Amblers, or to the legend about Brass Castle. Besides, I told him in confidence."

"Had Mr. Damerel stipulated that?"

"No. There was no sort of secrecy about it, really, but I thought Wilfred might prefer it that way."

"I see. Then you don't think—"

"I'm quite sure," said Father O'Malley again.

"And you didn't speak of the journal to anybody else?"

"I did not."

"Thank you, Father. There's just one other thing. . . did you write out the transcription for Mr. Damerel, or have it typed?"

"It was typed for me by another parishioner. . . a girl called Elsie Sweeney."

"*What?*"

"Elsie Sweeney. Is there anything odd about that, Mr. Maitland?"

"No, of course. . . did you swear her to secrecy, too?"

"There was no need. Elsie wasn't interested enough in the story to want to talk about it."

"Then I won't trouble you any further. I'm very grateful."

"I can't see that I've been very much help to you. Don't forget," said Father O'Malley, jovial again, "to let me know when you find the treasure."

"I won't," Antony promised, and replaced the receiver and went back to the fire. Bill gave him an odd look.

"What made you so excited?"

"The transcript of Hugh Ambler's journal was typed by a girl called Elsie Sweeney," said Antony impressively.

"What of it?"

"Don't you remember? It was a Mr. Sweeney who borrowed Clough's *History* from the library. . . the first time it had been out in years."

"Oh!" said Bill, and thought about it, frowning.

"First they went to Burntside Hall, and then she put them right about the story and they came here."

Jenny said slowly, "But that means—doesn't it— that you're almost certainly right that somebody is after the treasure."

"Let's say it increases the probability."

"It explains a lot," said Bill. "But if you're trying to make it explain Seth Dodgson's death as well—"

"What makes you think that?" asked Antony evasively.

"I could hear your half of the conversation," Bill told him. "I know you disclaimed, but it didn't sound too convincing."

"Yes. . . well. . . I wondered, that's all."

"Nonsense," said Bill forthrightly. "It was obviously something to do with the black market. . . that kind of violence. The truck you saw—"

Jenny leaned forward. "But we think it might be the same people," she said. Bill turned and stared at her.

"Not you, too, Jenny."

"Don't we, Antony?"

"It was your idea, love. I wouldn't say you're wrong."

"You're as mad as he is," said Bill despairingly. Bess laughed, and they all looked at her, and Jenny thought, she's been so quiet I've hardly got to know her at all.

"If you only knew," Bess said, a little abashed at having attracted so much attention, "how good it is to think about something that has nothing to do with what happened to Hester."

That was probably why Bill gave the subject a more patient hearing, when later Antony returned to it. But first there was the telephone call from the police. . . .

It turned out to be Sergeant Holroyd asking for Antony. "I just wanted to find out, Mr. Maitland, how sure you are of the number you gave us for the truck you saw."

Antony hesitated. "Well. . . sure enough. I wrote it down at the time."

"No second thoughts about it?"

"No," said Antony, and couldn't resist adding, "Why?"

Holroyd alone was much more talkative than Holroyd accompanying his superior officer. "It's rather a pity," he said. "You see, that number isn't in use anymore. It belonged to a car that was registered in 1930, and that went to the scrap yard three years back."

"Well, but. . .that's interesting in itself, isn't it?"

"It might be," said Holroyd with belated caution. "If you're sure you aren't mistaken."

"I don't think so," said Antony, feeling, of course, as soon as the question was raised, anything but confident. Holroyd, however, seemed quite satisfied, and thanked him and hung up. Antony turned from the telephone to find that Mrs. Dibb had come in for the tea things and was standing in her favorite place near the kitchen door with the tray balanced on the corner of the sideboard.

"Norman just got in," she remarked, addressing them all impartially. And then, "I'm wondering, Mr. Cleveland, if you'd mind him staying over to Ferrenscross for a day or two. Mrs. Dodgson could put him up, and it might make her pull herself together like, if she had something to do."

Bill said, "Yes, of course, Mrs. Dibb, that'll be all right."

Jenny said sympathetically, "I suppose she's awfully upset."

"Well, you see, it wasn't just t'shock, Mrs. Maitland, it was along of her finding him like that." Mrs. Dibb was obviously in no hurry to start the washing up.

"Did she. . .I didn't know she found him."

"She told Norman all about it," said Mrs. Dibb tolerantly. "Not once, mind you, but every time he went near her, all day. That's why I thought. . .she didn't really ought to be left alone."

"No, poor woman." Bill didn't seem to be going to put the question that was in all their minds, and Antony was just resigning himself to leaving his curiosity unsatisfied, when it became apparent that Mrs. Dibb had every intention of rounding out her story.

"Horrible, it was," she said, with the innocent relish of one who has never done anything more blameworthy than wring a chicken's neck. "She heard this truck stop in the road, and then after a minute or two it started up again. And she thought she'd best call Seth in to his dinner before anyone else came wanting him, but it wasn't quite ready so she waited a few minutes, and then she went out. And there he was, lying just outside t'mistal door, and his head cracked like an eggshell, and the blood—" At that point she caught sight of Bess's expression and stopped, folding her lips tightly on whatever else she had been about to say.

Antony glanced around at the others. . . Bill was impassive, as might have been expected, Jenny looked troubled, but not particularly horrified, but Bess looked as if she was going to be sick. He said into the silence, "Does she remember what time it was?"

"Ten past twelve exactly. She told Norman that's something she'll never forget. . . looking at t'clock, and then going out and finding him."

"So that's how the police knew so exactly when he died."

"That's how, Mr. Maitland. It must have been them as was in t'truck as did it," said Mrs. Dibb, looking from one of them to the other for agreement. "And why anyone should want to do a thing like that. . . . But there's nowt so queer as folk, is there?" she concluded, picking up the tray, which Antony took to be a sort of general absolution for the follies of mankind.

It was only after both these matters—Sergeant Holroyd's telephone call and Mrs. Dibb's revelations—had been thoroughly aired that Antony took the conversation back to the treasure hunt. "I forgot to ask you about Edward Ryder," he said.

"What about him?" asked Bill.

"He's the only other person Father O'Malley told about the journal."

"Well, I don't see . . . for one thing he's about a hundred and fifty, from all I've heard. For another, if somebody was acting on his instructions, they wouldn't have made a false cast at Burntside Hall."

"For that matter," said Bess, "if Elsie Sweeney had told them about the journal they'd have come straight here, wouldn't they?"

"What I think happened," said Antony, encouraged by Bill's forbearance, "is that first they saw a reference to the treasure in Ryder's newspaper article, then they went to the library—or rather Mr. Sweeney did—and found that it was reputed to be buried at Burntside Hall; and it was only afterward that Elsie mentioned—to her father, uncle, brother, whatever he is—that Clough was wrong and the real hiding place was at Brass Castle."

"If she told them about the journal they'll be doubly sure there's something to be found, because I don't suppose they know about Professor Micklefield's expedition," said Bill. "Another thing, they'll think it's information exclusive to themselves." And Jenny, who had already thought that out for herself, was made doubly uneasy by this voicing of her fears. "We may even," went on Bill, lightly, not believing it in the slightest, "have to withstand a siege."

But that was before it began to snow.

## 12

THE SNOW STARTED soon after midnight, and by the time Norman set off for Ferrenscross with Laddie at his heels, and Bill pumped up the Tilley lamp and went along to the mistal to start the milking, it was already lying about three inches deep. The evening milking and feeding time proved more difficult; there were drifts against the door of the farrowing pen, and the troughs in the field and in the garth behind the house had to be emptied before they could be used. The cows had accepted their incarceration contentedly enough; indeed, the mistal was a warm and pleasant shelter against a cruel wind. But the pigs, after various experiments conducted earlier in the day, apparently to ascertain if there was still solid ground under the blanket of white that was spread around them, had retreated sulkily into their various sleeping quarters and sang for their supper at least an hour before the appointed time.

Bess went over to Stavethorpe Hall after breakfast and returned in the early afternoon, even then walking with difficulty through the deepening snow. Cyril, she said, was delighted with the news of her engagement to Bill, and would come to Brass Castle to deliver his congratulations in person as soon as he could; just now he was up to his eyes in work—the storm made everything difficult. Bill seemed pleased with the message, but Jenny, with unaccustomed skepticism, remarked later to her husband that she doubted if it had been given in quite that form. Antony had been shut up in the office with his books all day, after reaching the conclusion that morning that he was less help than hindrance when it came to the routine work of the farm. Now he was piling his books together in case Bill wanted the desk later on, and sorting his notes, preparatory to emerging for a late tea, but he looked up and frowned at Jenny, taking her words more seriously than she had intended.

"Why don't you believe it, love?"

"I don't quite know. I suppose it's because Mr. Thornton didn't want Bess to stay here in the first place. Perhaps he guessed what would happen."

"I still can't see why he should object."

"No," said Jenny doubtfully.

"You're not still thinking—"

"Of course not." She didn't wait for him to finish. "But it isn't long since his wife died; I expect he's feeling lonely. And he's used to Bess. I could quite understand if he didn't want her to leave home just yet."

"I don't suppose Mrs. Clayton and Bob are much company," Antony agreed. "Anyway, I don't see what difference it can make. He isn't her guardian, or anything like that."

"All the same," said Jenny, shifting her ground, "I wish there wasn't all this talk."

Antony frowned again, this time down at the scrawled notes that were the only concrete evidence of his day's labor. "It will pass," he said. "Meanwhile, Bill's happy."

"Not too happy to care if he heard anything."

"Perhaps not. But it's very unlikely . . . anyway, he's heard the worst already. Don't worry, love." And, in fact, as Jenny would have been the first to admit, it was difficult to worry when you saw Bill and Bess together.

It stopped snowing in the late evening, but Mrs. Dibb shook her head in a foreboding way when Bill remarked optimistically that that was the end of that. There were a few flakes swirling down when he went out first thing next morning into the darkness, but it was snowing steadily again by the time he went in to breakfast, and this time it showed no sign of relenting. The wind was piling up the drifts, and Bess didn't venture out beyond the farmyard. By nightfall it was obvious that even if they got the milk out in the morning, no lorry would be able to make it to the collecting point in High Lane. Bill took the setback philosophically, merely remarking that if the weather didn't let up before all the churns he had on hand were full, the pigs were in for a treat.

It didn't come to that, though the sky continued gray, the wind went on blowing, and the snow came down intermittently for several days. Looking across the fields there was an unbroken expanse of white, the dry stone walls no longer visible, and the telegraph poles not much more than half their usual height. In the farmyard the snow was piled high where they had shoveled it to make the necessary paths to the barn, to the mistal, to the dairy, to the pigsties, and Bill had an extra digging job to do to keep feeding places clear for the pigs. But by Friday word had gone out that a bulldozer had cut out a path to the top of the Edge, and that a depot had been set up there where feeding stuffs could be dumped by the local supplier, and milk taken for collection. Luckily there was an old sledge in the barn that was quite serviceable, and, except for Stavethorpe Hall, Brass Castle was the farm with the least distance to traverse to this depot. Some of the moor farmers had to come for miles to bring their churns and pick up supplies of feed. The bulldozer spent each night at the top of the Edge with its engine running, and the driver lodged with Mrs. Clayton and walked up to it each morning. As it turned out, that arrangement went on for weeks, but that Friday, the seventeenth of January, no one knew how many blizzards were still to come. Mrs. Dibb was a provident woman, and in that remote district they were allowed to keep up to three months' rations in hand, so with the flour bin full and their own bacon and ham and salt pork, and the hens still laying, they were in no immediate danger of running short.

The inquest on Seth Dodgson's death had commenced on the Wednesday, and been adjourned for lack of witnesses...even the very necessary witness as to identity. Antony thought he might have managed the six-mile walk into Great Allerton, though certainly it would have been difficult, but there was no question of Mrs. Dodgson being able to get there, and he was glad enough not to have to make the attempt. Norman reported by telephone—the telephone really came into its own in those days—that all was going well at Ferrenscross...as well as could be expected.

So they settled down into a routine, which was the only way to get through the extra work Norman's absence and the adverse weather conditions entailed. Antony, unable to do much to help, put in more hours in the office than he had done for days past, though he would have been the first to admit, if anyone had thought to ask him, that his mind was often very far from the well-trodden paths of the law. Of the four of them, it was he whose normal activities were the most curtailed, and he was often hard put to it to conceal his irritation with this state of affairs. Jenny wondered whether to ask him if he would like to go home as soon as the road was open, but then she thought better of it. Anyway, though the subject of both treasure hunt and murders seemed to have been shelved by common consent, she was pretty sure what he would say. Bess appeared very content, though she grew rather quiet again as the days wore on. As for Bill, he seemed to thrive on difficulties.

That was the position on Friday evening. The day's work was done, it wasn't quite suppertime, and they were all gathered around the living-room fire. Bill and Jenny were quite frankly somnolent, Bess was embroidering a tea cloth that had originally been intended as a present for Hester Thornton... it was beautiful work, and the colors had been chosen with an artist's eye. As for Antony, he was trying to read *Wuthering Heights* as a change from Carpenter's *Principles of the Law of Real Property*, and not finding it much easier going. Being cut off from the library, he had to rely on what was on the bookshelves, and he was just about to demand an explanation from Bill as to what a set of the Brontës was doing among the adventure stories that were his usual relaxation and the farming books that were there for reference, when there came a loud rapping on the door.

Bess raised her head from her work, Jenny opened her eyes and blinked in the lamplight, Bill said, "What the devil?" And then, as he came more nearly awake, "Nobody would come calling on a night like this." Antony placed his book, face downward, on the sofa beside him.

"The road's open now to the top of Stavethorpe Edge," he said.

"Even so—"

"Well, one of us had better see who it is," said Antony, making no move to go. Bill came to his feet unwillingly, crossed the room and pulled open the door. A blast of cold air surged into the room. From where he was sitting Antony could see a shortish, square-built man on the step outside.

"Mr. Cleveland?"

"That's right."

"I hear," said the newcomer, "you're wanting to sell."

Bill was puzzled, and it sounded in his voice. It hardly seemed the moment to choose. . . . "I've nothing ready for market at the moment," he said.

"Not your stock, Mr. Cleveland. The farm." The visitor wasn't a local man; a southerner, Antony thought—an educated voice, but not without an accent of some sort that he couldn't quite identify.

"I most certainly do not." Bill was still sore on that point; you could guess that he was scowling.

"That's a pity. Perhaps we could come in and talk it over." As he spoke, two other men moved out of the shadows into the circle of lamplight that spilled from the open door. "We've come a long way," he added. If his tone was meant to be persuasive, it was a dismal failure. There was a chilliness about it that the surface friendliness couldn't quite hide. Antony got up and took his favorite position, with his back to the hearth but a little to one side of the fire, and was aware as he did so of the cold breath of fear. Something more tangible now than what he had felt in How Gill nearly a fortnight before, and even more compelling. The man was dangerous. His instinct was to push past Bill, and shut the door in the face of the man outside, and slam home the bolt, but how could he ever explain? He stood very still, and did not know that Jenny was watching him.

"There's nothing to talk about," Bill was saying. But he backed away a little, obligingly, and held the door more widely open. "You'd better come in and get warmed up before you go."

"That's kind of you." The first man came past him into the room, and his two companions followed him. "But it's early days to talk about going yet," he went on, as Bill closed the door and kicked the roll of blanket that served as a draft excluder into place.

It was quite obvious to Antony, if only from the woodenness of his expression, that Bill was becoming ruffled. He said, ignoring the last remark, "How did you get here, anyway?"

"It's quite easy going up to the top of Stavethorpe Edge, though the snow's blowing across the road in places. From there we came across the fields; the jeep's just outside the gate. You can go almost anywhere with a four-wheel drive."

"Yes, of course." Bill wasn't really interested, though he had raised the question himself. "I can offer you coffee, if that would suit you. I'm afraid I haven't anything stronger."

"That's real hospitality for you," said the stranger. The joviality of his voice rang as false as the earlier persuasiveness had done. His eyes were moving around the room, cataloging its contents, taking account, one by one, of its occupants.

Jenny said, "I'll tell Mrs. Dibb," and one of the men who had not so far spoken moved a little, as if to bar the way to the kitchen door. He was a taller man than his leader, probably in his late forties, with black, curly hair, a round, good-looking face, and an easier, more friendly manner.

"Not so fast, miss," he said, and Antony bent down to lay a restraining hand on Jenny's arm; she sank back into her corner of the sofa again, looking puzzled.

Bill said, letting his anger show, "I've no wish to force anything on you, but I think—"

"Business before pleasure," the first man said sententiously. He had finished his stocktaking now. "Come back to the fire, Mr. Cleveland; you'll catch cold over there by the door."

"I've told you—"

"So you have. Come back to the fire," he re-peated, his tone only a little more insistent than before. And then, with ill-feigned concern, "You all look so comfortable, it's a shame to interrupt you."

"I'm only sorry you've had your journey for nothing," said Bill, obviously not meaning a word of it.

"I wouldn't say that."

"I would." Bill sounded grim. But he moved past the visitors to join the group by the fire again, and made one last attempt to treat the situation as nor-mal. "There are chairs by the table, if you want to sit down."

"Not just at the moment. Where's Norman Dibb?" the other man asked abruptly.

"If it's Norman you want—"

"I said, *where is he?*" There was an underlying viciousness in his tone that made the short hairs prickle at the back of Antony's neck.

He said, before Bill could reply, "Hadn't we bet-ter introduce ourselves?" but he was thinking, so my instinct was right, and I'd have done better to follow it.

"No need. I know who you are," the spokesman told him.

"Do you, though?"

"You don't know it all, Ted," said the third man, breaking his silence. "Joe was driving; he wouldn't recognize him, but that's the young bloke what was leaving Ferrenscross last Saturday." He was a southerner, too, a cockney by the sound of it. A small man, thin faced, younger than either of his companions.

Ted said nothing; only his eyes became more in-tent. The man by the kitchen door said, "Shut up, Sidney." It sounded like a routine protest, one which he didn't expect to bear any fruit.

"Too late for that," said Ted.

Bill exclaimed, as though enlightened, before Antony could do anything to stop him, "So you were the chaps at Ferrenscross when Seth Dodgson died."

"And if we were?"

"It makes me wonder," said Bill bluntly, "which of you killed him."

That produced a moment of silence; a nasty, uncomfortable silence, Antony thought it. He said, because anything seemed preferable to letting it continue, "Oddly enough, Bill, I don't think any of them did."

"That," said Ted, "is perceptive of you. We'd no reason to want him dead. I take it, however, you told the police—"

"It didn't help them. They've already discovered the number plate was a fake."

"You reassure me," said Ted ironically. His hand went to the pocket of his overcoat, and emerged again holding a revolver. An army .38, from the look of it. "May I return the compliment by assuring you that I don't want to hurt any of you, unless I must." It was queer, thought Antony—calm, now that his worst fears were realized—how clearly the threat was implicit in his words.

Bess shrank back a little into the depths of her chair; Jenny gave a gasp that might have meant anything from fright to pure surprise; Bill said angrily, "I don't know what all this is about—"

"Don't you?" He didn't even attempt to hide, now, the coldness of his voice.

Antony said, because he didn't want another silence to develop, "What I'd like to know—and it can't do any harm to tell me—is, which of you is Mr. Sweeney?"

This time it was the black-haired man who replied, saying softly, "How did you know my name?"

"By putting two and two together. My friends would tell you I'm just as likely to make it twenty-two, but in this case—"

"Joe Sweeney, at your service," said the black-haired man. "But you haven't told me—"

"All in good time, Joe," said the man called Ted. His eyes were fixed on Antony's face. "If you're so clever, can you also tell us what we're doing here?"

"You said you wanted to buy the farm."

"That wasn't quite true."

"No, I see. A ruse to gain admission."

"Or artifice," said Ted. "Whichever you like."

"It seems to come to the same thing. But as to what you're doing here," said Antony, "I'd be willing to make a guess. You're treasure hunting, aren't you? Of course, I don't know why you've chosen this particular moment—"

"Don't you?" asked Ted again, dryly.

"Unless, of course, the police are getting a bit too close for comfort in their black-market investigations, in which case I expect you want to make a killing and depart rapidly for other spots."

"I don't like this," said Sidney unexpectedly.

This time it was Ted who said, "Shut up!" without turning around. "If I tell you you're near the truth," he added to Antony, "it will perhaps serve to emphasize the fact that we'll stop at nothing."

His suavity was beginning to rasp on Antony's nerves. "It seems rather hard on Joe, doesn't it?" he said, improvising freely. "You're not local men, you and Sidney, but he's got a home and family that he'll have to leave, and perhaps a job, as well." He broke off, because Joe was laughing silently, and even Sidney, less at ease than the other two, gave a snigger.

"No family," Joe said. (What did that make Elsie, then? His niece, perhaps, or his sister.) "And no job worth having."

"That's a pity," said Antony, and meant it. But there was no profit in this; the three men presented, for the moment, at least, a united front. And it didn't seem that anything he could say would serve to drive a wedge between them. "Have you got a fence lined up, too?"

"A contact of mine in . . . well, never mind that. Abroad," said Ted, who also seemed to be finding the situation amusing. "If you've an eye for an opportunity, the army has a way of extending your horizons."

"I wouldn't argue about that."

"No, I don't suppose you would. You realize, of course," he went on, letting his eyes move slowly from one of them to another, "that we are unlikely to be interrupted." And that was only too true. "Which brings me back to the question I asked you some time ago: where is Norman Dibb?"

It didn't seem a point worth quibbling about; they could find out only too easily that Norman wasn't at home. "He's at Ferrenscross," said Antony, making a virtue of necessity. "Looking after things until they get somebody to take Seth Dodgson's place."

Ted nodded, as if he found this reasonable, but he wasn't taking any chances. "Have a look around, Joe," he suggested. Joe Sweeney disappeared without a word through the door that led to the kitchen. "And you, Sidney, take a look upstairs."

"Where *are* the stairs?" asked Sidney plaintively.

Unfortunately, even now Ted didn't bother to turn his head. The gun was steady in his hand, aimed at a point roughly midway between Antony and Bill, and it hadn't been only the occupants of the room he had taken in during that first, slow appraisal. "Try the door over there that looks as if it might be a cupboard," he recommended. A moment later Sidney was padding up the stone staircase, whose treads were worn by generations of use.

"And now," said Ted, becoming businesslike and turning his attention again to Bill, "what do you know about this 'treasure'?" He emphasized the word as if it pleased him, but also he was amused by it.

This time Antony succeeded in catching Bill's eye, and shook his head ever so slightly. There was no need for more . . . when they had been at school together they had perfected the art of wordless communication. "A rumor, unsubstantiated, that it is buried here," he said.

"That's where you're wrong," Ted told him, for some reason pleased to be demonstrating his own greater knowledge. "The man that hid it left a record . . . that chap Damerel knows, but I don't suppose he's telling. That's why he tried to buy this place last spring, and will be after it again when it comes on the market."

"There was a treasure hunt here before the war. Didn't Seth Dodgson ever tell you? They searched pretty thoroughly."

Ted laughed. "Even if I believed you, they didn't know what *I* know," he said.

"Where is it, then?" asked Antony, spreading his hands in a gesture that disclaimed any acquaintance with the contents of Hugh Ambler's journal.

"In the dairy," said Ted, still smug.

"I was told the other lot looked there, among other places."

"Who do you think you're kidding?"

No good trying to persuade him. . . . "So you're going to dig for it," Antony said.

"We are."

"Quite a big job."

"We've got all the time in the world. Even if the weather breaks, this lot won't go away in a hurry." Ted was on top of the situation, and enjoying it. "You're not overlooked, and if anybody sees a light from the other side of the valley, they're not likely to walk two miles on a night like this to investigate it." Antony allowed a trace of dejection to appear in his manner.

"I suppose you've already identified the dairy," he said. This time he didn't risk a glance in Bill's direction.

"That was easy. . .the building on the left of the cowshed." Antony looked more gloomy than ever, and hoped this was sufficient to convince Ted that he was right. Better they dug up the present dairy than turned their attention to the old one, which was now the larder. It would get them out of the house for a time, give him a chance to think of a plan. As it was, as long as Ted kept his distance and the gun in his hand, there wasn't a thing to be done. Bill, he hoped, could see that as well as he could. Even if their position hadn't been made so much more vulnerable by Jenny and Bess being present. . . he became conscious of the pain in his shoulder, which for the last half hour he had forgotten; a disheartening reminder of his own disability.

Joe and Sidney returned from their errands simultaneously. "No one upstairs," said Sidney.

Joe added, "Just the old lady in the kitchen. I've locked the back door, she can't get out." He was tossing the heavy key in his hand. "And I've found just the place to put them. . .a little room off the kitchen, used as a pantry. It has a heavy door, and a bolt on the outside."

."That's very satisfactory."

"It isn't satisfactory at all!" Bill came explosively back into the conversation. "You can't put the girls in there. . .they'll freeze to death."

"I can't help thinking you underrate them, Mr. Cleveland. In any case, that is hardly my concern."

"How long?"

"One day. . .two days." Ted was vague. Antony

was aware of an increasing desire to smash his self-confidence, if only he could have thought of a way. But it was Bill who took up the argument.

"Well, there's the question of food. . .for you, as well as us."

"I feel sure something can be arranged. . . amicably," said Ted. The slightest movement of the gun underlined his meaning.

"*And* the stock," said Bill. "And if you're going to remind me you aren't the R.S.P.C.A., let me tell you there'll be an unholy racket in the morning if the pigs aren't fed on time."

"That, too—"

"It'll concern you all right if the bulldozer driver comes over to see what's up." Bill was getting angrier by the minute. . .too angry to have any regard for what might have been good tactics.

Ted said gently, "I'm obliged to you, of course, for pointing it out, but I still think Joe's idea is a good one. The other matters can be dealt with as they arise." The gun had moved now, and was pointing squarely at Jenny's head. "If you'll be good enough to precede me. . .Mr. Cleveland. . . and your friend. . .and the young lady who, from all I hear, must be Miss Foster." Bill gave one glance at Antony, a compound of wrath and helplessness, and then moved obediently toward the kitchen. But Antony was looking at Jenny.

"Take it easy, love," he advised, and saw in her answering smile how desperately afraid she was, so that he was suddenly furiously angry and had to struggle consciously against it, not to let it blind him to the wisdom of doing exactly as he was told. It was as hard as anything he had done in his life, to turn away from her, to follow Bill. Joe Sweeney had gone before them and was holding open the larder door; it was no surprise to see that he, too, held a revolver, though he didn't look as at home with it as Ted did.

Mrs. Dibb was standing, hesitating, outrage in every line of her body, until Bill said quietly, "You'd better do as they say."

"Mr. Cleveland!" she protested.

"Or somebody may get hurt." The starch went out of her then when she saw he meant what he said. She followed him without another word, stooping, as they all had to do, under the low lintel.

Coming from the warmth and mellow light of the kitchen, the larder was pitch-dark and bitterly cold. Antony's groping hand found Jenny's, and he pulled her close to him, feeling her shiver, and putting his left arm around her shoulders. Nobody spoke for a moment, so that they all heard the bolt shoot home, though it was only Jenny who felt Antony stiffen, and heard the hiss of his indrawn breath. Then Bill said in a voice that was studiously matter-of-fact, "What do we do now?"

## 13

NOBODY ANSWERED FOR A MOMENT, and then Antony said thoughtfully, "I think that first we ought to explain to Mrs. Dibb—"

"Aye, I'd be glad if someone'd do that." They all knew that grim tone. So they told her, in chorus and confusingly, everything that had happened ever since that surprising knock on the front door; and it was a tribute to her intelligence that she seemed to grasp, at least, the bare bones of the story. "Well, are we going to stand here in the dark, then?" she demanded when they had finished. "There's candles on t'shelf, and if you haven't got a box of matches in your pocket, Mr. Cleveland, I'll be surprised."

The candles took a bit of finding in the dark, but there seemed to be a good supply, so they lighted two and set them to burn on the stone slabs that stood two-and-a-half feet high around three walls of the little room. The old dairy was about twelve feet by twelve, built of undressed stone right into the side of the hill. Both the shelves and the flagged floor had a wonderful patina, brown like a pebble, which according to Mrs. Dibb was the result of hundreds of years of spilled milk. Just at the moment, of course, none of them was in a mood to appreciate aesthetic values; to them it was an uncomfortable place, not only bitingly cold, but damp as well, and eerie in the flickering candlelight.

"It's ironic, isn't it," said Antony, looking around

him, "that they should shut us up in the very place Hugh Ambler said the treasure was hidden?"

Bill was inclined to be short with him. "I can't see what good you did, sending them off to dig in the wrong place. It isn't as if the treasure is really here—they were welcome to look—and then they might have found a warmer place for us to stay."

"They might," Antony agreed. "But at least they're out of the house now . . . or will be as soon as they've got the lamps pumped up."

"I can't see what good that does us," said Bess. She might be forgiven for sounding a little waspish; her teeth were chattering with the cold. Bill took off his jacket and draped it around her shoulders, and Antony shrugged out of his, too, and handed it to Jenny. He wasn't quite sure how Mrs. Dibb would go on, but it seemed likely that she was wearing more layers of clothing than the girls were. Certainly her dress was of a thicker material.

"It means if we try to get out they won't hear us," he said.

He meant his tone to be consoling, but even in his own ears it sounded sharp. Bess gave a kind of snort that conveyed only too clearly her contempt for the suggestion, and Jenny asked in a hurry, her instinct to keep the peace operating even under these adverse conditions, "Yes, but what can we do?"

"That seems to me to be Bill's department," Antony told her. "As a practical man, Bill—"

"We can't do anything with the door," said Bill, who had been examining it while they were talking. "It's set right into the recess between the two rooms, so we can't lift it off its hinges, and with that heavy bolt outside nothing short of a battering ram would shift it."

"Well, we've got to think of something," said Antony reasonably, and added, when Bill made no immediate reply, "Have you thought what's likely to happen when they give up in despair and leave?''

"If they're going to dig up the whole floor of the new dairy that won't be for some time," Bill pointed out.

Jenny said, in a voice that was carefully expressionless, "Do you think they'll kill us?''

"I didn't mean that.''

"No, but they might...don't you think? They know that we know that they were at Ferrenscross on Saturday. You actually saw the truck, Antony...they know that, too.''

"I don't think that need worry you, love.''

"But it does. I didn't mind Joe and Sidney so much, but the man they called Ted was...horrible.''

"In a different league altogether from the other two," Antony agreed.

"And yet," said Bill, "he's fallen for a tale of buried treasure.''

"That doesn't surprise me." Antony told him. "Do you know how much has been spent over the years on abortive treasure hunts...and by so-called hardheaded businessmen, at that? These chaps don't stand to lose anything, and what they gain may be incalculable...or so they think.''

"They murdered Seth Dodgson," said Jenny, returning to her original thesis.

"I meant it when I said I didn't think so. It wasn't just policy. They probably had some black-market dealings with him, and that's why they went to Ferrenscross. In any case, our evidence on that point won't be much good to the police if the birds have flown.''

"But—" said Bill.

Antony said, "Precisely," very much as Sir Nicholas might have done, without waiting for his conclusion, and added, in case any of the others hadn't followed his train of thought, "They've got to give themselves time to fly.''

"You mean, they're likely to leave us...shut up...in here." Bess's voice had gone up a notch or two, in contrast to Jenny's, which seemed to grow quieter as she became more frightened. Even at that moment there was a part of Antony's mind that registered, and appreciated, the fact that they were neither of them having hysterics. Mrs. Dibb continued, imperturbable or apparently so, but he would have expected nothing else.

"That's exactly what I mean," he said. "And, apart from the risk of pneumonia—"

"We might starve to death," said Bess, and gave rather a shaky laugh. "That would be ironic, too, wouldn't it? To starve to death in a larder."

Antony didn't feel equal to commenting on that. He said, "If the door's no good—and I agree with you about that, Bill—we've got to think of something else."

"Well, the window's no use, either," said Bill, holding up one of the candles so that they could see for themselves, and swearing as the hot wax spilled onto his hand. "Even Jenny couldn't get through it."

Which, indeed, was obvious. The window was a tiny, unglazed aperture, set high in the wall to be above ground level, and sealed for the winter by a wooden shutter that didn't fit very well. A five-year-old child might possibly have made use of it, if sufficiently agile, but nothing larger. Antony stared up at it and then said, so slowly that it was obvious he was picking his words, "Do you remember, Bill, telling me that you were going to have a ditch for drainage dug right around the back of the house once the winter's over?"

"I do, of course," said Bill, rather shortly. "But I don't see—"

Bill stared at him. "God Almighty!" he said after a moment in an awed voice. "So there may be a way out after all."

"You can't pull down the wall with your bare hands," Antony objected, changing his tune now that he had got Bill thinking, he hoped, along the right lines.

"No, but—" Bill was eager now. "Forget about the wall, that suggestion's worse than useless. But that corner where the plaster fell, and I fixed a bit of plasterboard over the hole. I could get that off again easily enough."

"What would that do for us?"

"We could get up into the underdrawing. Look here, what do you know about the roof?"

"It's the original, isn't it? Bloody great stone slabs like paving stones."

"That's right. They're fixed in place with wooden pegs; if we could take those out we could heave one of the slabs out of the way."

"But can we move the pegs?"

"Easily; some of them have even fallen out over the years. It's the sheer weight of the roof that really holds it in place."

"Good. But what about noise?"

Bill thought for a moment. "All right, then. If we raise one slab a little, and slide the one underneath it up...the top one will hold the bottom one in place. I'll need your help, Antony. Can you—?"

"I'll manage." He would have done more than that to get away from the enclosed space, away from the memory of the bolted door. "How much room will it give us?"

"Room for Jenny to squeeze through, with luck. The roof's at ground level at the back there, so once she's out it wouldn't be difficult." Bill was already working at the piece of plasterboard as he spoke. "Then she can go around the other end of the house, and come back in and release us."

It wasn't, of course, quite as simple as it sounded, but then, none of them thought it would be. Bill got up fairly nimbly into the underdrawing, using the shelves as a rather inconveniently placed ladder; for Antony, following him with one arm out of action took on some of the quality of a nightmare. He managed it at last, and in spite of the cold he was sweating. After that things went more smoothly, though because of the precautions they had to take against making a noise, and because of the cramped quarters, it seemed an age before the job was done. They had made an aperture the width of the roof stone, and about nine inches deep, and the candle they were using flared and spluttered in the draft.

Antony went down into the dairy again before Jenny went up to take his place. "You know what to do, love."

"Yes, I think so." Jenny was kicking off her slippers, which would be worse than useless in the deep snow. "If I can, I come around and let you out; if not, if they've left someone on guard in the house, or if they've locked the door, I go across to Stavethorpe to get help."

"Take care of yourself."

"I will." It was Jenny's turn to add, "Don't worry." She was already climbing up to join Bill, reaching up to take his hand and pulling herself up to join him more easily than either of the men had done. Antony thought her calm had a brittle surface, and would shatter only too easily, but he let her go without protest, and without further admonition. There was nothing else to be done.

A couple of minutes later Bill's legs reappeared through the hole in the plaster, and he let himself down to join them. "She's gone," he reported. He leaned over toward one of the remaining candles to consult his watch. "Do you realize it's only just after ten o'clock?"

Bess sounded surprised. "I thought half the night had passed." And Mrs. Dibb said, "I wonder what happened to t'stew I had in t'oven,'' which wasn't really irrelevant. Antony said nothing, and wished the others would be silent, too; his ears were alert for any sound. But when one came it was more quickly than he would have believed possible . . . the pulling of the bolt and the gentle easing of the door open by Jenny, because it sometimes squeaked.

"There's nobody around," she said, whispering. "There are lights in the dairy, and I heard voices and some banging, but I don't know what they're doing."

"Never mind about that." Bill was across the kitchen already, pulling on his thigh boots, and he, too, spoke in a low voice. "I'll be off right away. Bolt the back door, in case that chap Sweeney still has the key in his pocket, and lock the front door behind me."

"You'd better have your jacket back," said Bess.

"All right. Go into the living room and get warm again, but don't turn up the lamp; they'll be less likely to hear you in there."

Jenny was there already, taking off her wet stockings and rubbing her feet and legs dry on a towel she had taken from the kitchen. Antony said, "I'll have your other pair of boots, Bill," and brought them with him into the living room, and sat down to pull them on.

"There's no need for two of us to go."

"I want to get the rotor arm off the jeep, then they'll be immobilized even if they get the wind up before relief gets here."

"It's an idea, but don't you think they may turn nasty if they hear you?"

"I'll chance that. Get along, Bill. I'll follow in about five minutes."

"Ten," said Bill. "I still think they may hear you."

"All right then, ten." He pulled open the front door, as gently as Jenny had dealt with the one into the larder, and Bill slipped out past him without another word. The key turned in the heavy lock with no more than the faintest sound.

Bess moved nearer the fire, which had burned low now, but was still comfortingly warm after the damp chill of the old dairy. "How long do you think it will take the police to get here?"

"Forty minutes. . . forty-five."

"Nearer an hour, probably," said Jenny. "Do you think," she added, still in the quiet voice he was beginning to recognize, "there'll be any shooting when they arrive?"

That idea had been worrying Antony for some time. He thought he could deal with the problem, though he didn't think Bill would have approved the method, but he couldn't think of any better reply than, "I don't know." Jenny glanced at him quickly, but, rather surprisingly, seemed satisfied with the answer. She looked up at Mrs. Dibb and patted the sofa beside her to encourage the older woman to sit down and relax. They all stayed in silence for a while, letting the warmth soak into them, and Antony wondered whether it might not have been better, after all, if they had all left the farm in a body. But Mrs. Dibb, who suffered from rheumatism, would have found the going difficult, particularly as far as the road, and however quiet they had tried to be there was more chance of five people being heard than one. On the whole, perhaps, Bill's decision had been the right one; but he wished the time would pass. The ten-minute wait—nearer eight minutes now—seemed to stretch before him like an infinity of time; and when it was over he knew he had to make up his mind. . . .

Jenny said at last, "It's twenty past ten, Antony."

"Time for me to go?"

"It's exactly ten minutes."

"I see." Perhaps they wouldn't recognize his reluctance, or would think it no more than a disinclination to leave the warmth of the room, instead of . . . what was it, after all? He couldn't say "fear of the unknown," that was part of the trouble, wasn't it? He had seen Ted and recognized him for what he was . . . a dangerous man with a streak of viciousness it wouldn't be too difficult to rouse.

He could stay where he was. So easy to change his mind; nobody would question the decision. Nobody but himself would ever know why he had refused the challenge, nobody would ever blame him. . . . He came to his feet and smiled down at Jenny. "Lock the door after me, love. And don't unlock it again until I get back, whatever you hear."

"Right." She gave him another of those quick, suspicious looks, but still she didn't say anything. Then she padded across, barefoot, to join him near the door.

II

TURN RIGHT along the front of the house, past the farrowing pens and up the garth, the way Jenny had come from the gap they had made in the roof. Plunging through the deep snow was like walking in a dream, with each step weighted, each harder to make than the one before. Up the garth, around the back of the house, past the rear of the dairy and the mistal. Over the wall, which he couldn't see, but it wasn't difficult to tell where it was because the drifts were deeper, almost waist high. This was the tricky part, because the pigs were good watchdogs, and he had to go right past the door of one of the pens. But if Bill could manage it . . . Bill, who—whatever other dangers he had encountered—had never had to walk silently in the shadows with the fear of discovery dogging his heels. . . .

There were sounds from the direction of the dairy, and he paused for a moment, trying to identify them. . . a sort of thumping sound, enough probably to cover any noise he might make, unless he was unforgivably clumsy. He could see the jeep now, or rather the shape of it. There must have been three inches of snow since Ted and his companions arrived; even the wheel tracks were obliterated, but the wind would have helped with that. He went up to the hood, and fumbled a little opening it. Carefully. . . but even so it gave a protesting shriek that set his heart beating faster. He stood still for an endless instant, but nothing happened, so he produced the flashlight he had brought with him and shone it on the engine, taking care to shade it as well as he could with his hand.

Mission accomplished. That was the first step; the second promised to be less easy. He moved around the front of the jeep to the field gate, and wondered whether it would be better to open it or to clamber over—which would make the least sound? In the end he opened it a crack and slipped through, keeping a hand on the latch until it was tight closed again.

Light was spilling out of the dairy from the open door. He moved a little closer and saw the Tilley lamp hanging from the center beam. With so bright an illumination they wouldn't be able to see him outside, unless he went right up to the doorway, and even then. . . .

He was about three paces from the door now. All three men were in their shirt-sleeves, but none of them seemed to be feeling the cold. Several of the flagstones that had been pried up were leaning against the wall, Ted and Joe were making a concerted attack upon another with a crowbar, and

Sidney seemed to be giving himself a breathing space, leaning on a spade. Two more spades were reared up against the wall, and a cold chisel and a sledgehammer, which presumably they had used to get a leverage on the first of the flags, were lying near them. The men's discarded coats were hanging on a piece of iron projecting conveniently from one wall—not too far from the door, another three paces, perhaps; but not so near as he would have liked. With any luck their armory would be back in the pockets again. Why not? They weren't expecting any interruption.

What he needed now was Bill's woodpile. He edged away, and around to the back of the mistal where the old cattle stalls awaited the saw. The snow was a help, really, deadening sound, and giving him light to see by. He selected a piece of two-by-four about eighteen inches long; heavy enough for the job he had in mind, not too heavy to handle.

Back to the dairy door. Sidney had gone back to work, and it was Ted who was standing back idle, watching Joe, who had the flagstone half raised, using a piece of timber as a fulcrum. The question was, could he throw straight enough with his left hand? But it was no use standing here and worrying about it; he had made up his mind—hadn't he—and now he had to go through with it.

So he flung his billet of wood at the Tilley lamp as hard as he could, and the result was just as he had hoped. The crash of the breaking glass was startling enough to immobilize Ted and his companions at least for an instant, and of course the mantel was shattered, too. The darkness blinded him for an instant, after staring straight into the light, but it seemed likely that the other men's eyes would take even longer to adjust. He lunged in the darkness toward the place where the coats were hanging, his groping hand found the cloth and he pulled them down, one after the other, and made for the door again. It wasn't until later that he had time to remember the startled cry Sidney had given, or the fact that Joe was swearing, or Ted's voice angrily demanding a flashlight. He was outside now, and his eyes were coming into their own again.

There wasn't a moment to be lost. He was fortunate again in finding a gun in the first coat he tried...Ted's .38, unless he was mistaken. It felt familiar to his hand. He dragged it free of the folds of material, and spun the cylinder to see, or rather to feel, if there were cartridges in all chambers. Luck was still with him. He cocked it, because he wanted to get his first shot in quickly, the rest of his haul went over the low wall into the kitchen garden, and he went back to the dairy again, a little to one side of the door, and fired a single shot across the opening.

"I shouldn't come out if I were you," he said into the sudden shocked silence that followed. Afterward he thought that it was the shot alone that convinced them he meant business; he had no idea that there was anything menacing about his tone of voice.

Jenny could have told him. She had come rushing out of the house when she heard the shot, with Bess just behind her, and Mrs. Dibb, who couldn't get up very quickly, bringing up the rear. The next few minutes were a pandemonium of question and answer, with confusion worse confounded by the angry recriminations of the men inside the dairy, who had become vocal again. He couldn't persuade any of the women to go indoors and stay there, though Mrs. Dibb disappeared for a few moments and came back with an armful of coats. Later he thought that their point of view was reasonable enough; at the time he could think only that the next forty minutes would be tricky, and that he didn't trust Ted an inch. But he never found out what would have happened if the treasure hunters had had time to formulate a plan; the police, surprisingly in the shape of Inspector Walton and Sergeant Holroyd, arrived not much more than ten minutes after he had fired his warning shot, and Bill with them, plowing across the fields in a Land Rover by the route the jeep must have taken earlier in the evening.

They took over the prisoners and the gun, and because they had only two pairs of handcuffs between them they put Ted in the middle and manacled Sidney to his right hand, and Joe Sweeney to his left. It didn't seem an altogether appropriate time to take detailed statements—what Bill had told them was enough for the present—so before long they went away, and Antony and Bill went back into the house to get warm again. There was also the matter of the dairy roof to deal with, but Bill seemed in no hurry to tackle that. He didn't even say anything to Antony about the measures he had taken to disarm Ted and Joe before he returned with reinforcements, which Antony had confidently expected would be the first item on the agenda, though he was pleased enough to find it was to be skipped altogether. So he made what explanations were needed by Jenny and Bess, which didn't take long—Mrs. Dibb had gone back to the kitchen to try to salvage the stew—and then turned to Bill, who hadn't sat down when the others did.

"You haven't told us, Bill, how you managed to get back with the police so quickly."

Bill took a moment to answer that, and his hesitation had the effect of fixing their attention, though from his expression that was the last thing he wanted to do. "They were already at Stavethorpe Hall when I got there. Walton and Holroyd and their driver," he said at last, and moved a few paces until he was standing by Bess's chair. "I'm sorry," he told her, but even now he couldn't bring himself to come directly to the point. "It seems they were just waiting for the road to be open before they came, but they didn't hear until this evening, and then they wanted to search the house and the buildings—"

Bess had twisted her head to look up at him. She had a strained expression, perhaps not to be wondered at after all that happened during the last few hours, but Antony thought it was more likely that she knew already what Bill was trying to say. "I'm sorry," he apologized again. "I don't like having to tell you this, Bess." And then, baldly, addressing a point somewhere over her head, "They've arrested Cyril."

"Oh, no!" Bess looked at him aghast. But when Bill bent down and tried to put an arm around her shoulders, she shuddered away from his touch and began to cry. Antony, watching, saw Bill straighten, and his troubled look, and thought it was time to take a hand. He didn't look at Jenny beside him on the sofa, but leaned forward with all his attention concentrated on the other girl.

"Bess," he said, and then, more insistently, "Bess." She raised her head, and he saw the tears on her cheeks, and Bill's expression, still more bewildered than hurt. "Didn't you expect that to happen?"

"Of course I didn't," she said. He would hardly have recognized her voice, it was so choked by crying. "I didn't think they'd ever find out for certain. I don't see *how* they found out."

Bill said too loudly, "Leave her alone," but when he sat down on the arm of her chair and tried to take her hand she pulled away from him almost petulantly. "You don't know what you're saying, Bess," he told her. And added to Antony, "Can't you see she's in a state of shock?"

"Yes, I think so. That's why she'll tell me." Bess was looking at him rather as a rabbit might look at a stoat. He paused long enough to think, what would happen if I leave it there? Would she marry Bill, and—if she's young enough to forget—would they one day be happy together? He didn't like playing the part of fate; he might lose Bill's friendship, and that was something he valued. But it was because they were friends that nothing less than the truth was good enough. "You knew all along, didn't you, Bess?"

"I—I guessed."

"The poison was in the gooseberry jam." That was a statement, not a question, and she answered it with renewed petulance.

"Of course it was! Every time she had some she was ill all over again. But I didn't know . . . I didn't *know*. So how could they, when the jam was all used up?" She broke off and looked at Jenny, and then at Bill; and perhaps it was only then that she realized, belatedly, the full import of what she had been saying. She covered her face with her hands and began to sob, quietly at first, and then with less restraint until she became almost hysterical.

It was left to Jenny, with Mrs. Dibb's assistance, to deal with that.

## 14

LATER, WHEN BESS had been put to bed with hot milk and a couple of aspirin tablets ("Just as if it was any ordinary day," said Jenny, as they went down the stairs), the other three gathered around the fire in the living room again, and Mrs. Dibb brought them bowls of rather overcooked stew and adjured them, inevitably, to eat it while it was hot. She had shown no surprise at anything that had happened that eventful evening, but Antony would have been very much surprised if she didn't know a good deal more than she would ever admit.

Bill hadn't said a word since he and Antony had been left alone while the two women persuaded Bess to go upstairs, and he had pushed his stew away untasted. Jenny said now, anxiously, "Do you think we ought to have called the doctor after all?"

He turned from his contemplation of the fire and said in a level tone, "Better not. Heaven knows what she would have said to him."

Jenny met his look, and asked the question that Antony had been afraid to put into words. "We're to keep silent, then?"

"If you will." Bill was finding more difficulty with his voice now. "I realize," he said, "that she didn't care for me at all. I suppose she thought it would help Cyril in some way, if she was known to be engaged to me."

"I'm afraid that's true," said Antony, finding his voice.

"Well, all right, then. But I couldn't bear to—to betray her."

"There's no question of that. What could we report, after all? A few wild words that she would deny when she was herself again. Better let it lie."

Bill turned to look at him. "It's too soon to expect me to thank you for letting me know the truth," he said bitterly.

Mrs. Dibb came in then, which saved Antony the necessity of replying. She exchanged their bowls of stew for cups of cocoa, but didn't comment upon the fact that none of them seemed to have much appetite.

When she had gone there was a long pause, while Bill seemed to be mesmerized by the fire again, but at last he said, "You were wrong about one thing, though. It wasn't for Hester Thornton's murder he was arrested—"

"I guessed that. It was because he killed Seth Dodgson, wasn't it?"

"Yes. I don't know what brought them to Stavethorpe, but when they searched the buildings they found a tire lever hidden in the straw of one of the mangers that aren't in use any longer. There were still traces of blood and hair."

"But he had an alibi," Jenny objected.

"I could give you a logical account of the two murders," Antony assured her, "but I have to admit that a good deal of it is guesswork. The only thing is, it does fit the facts."

"I never thought," said Bill, "I never thought it was possible that Cyril—" He broke off, as if the words had reminded him of the greater betrayal of trust, and then went on in the expressionless tone that Antony was beginning to dread to hear, "You'd better tell us, hadn't you?" Bill's anger, which he had been afraid of arousing, would have been no worse than this; but perhaps, after all, anything was better than letting the silence continue.

"Very well," he said, and got up to stand with his back to the fire, because it seemed to him that he could think better on his feet. "It all started with Father O'Malley, or that's what I think, because early last year he made a transcript of Hugh Ambler's journal. Cyril Thornton was one of the people Mr. Damerel told about it, and I expect he asked all the same questions I did, and heard that the treasure had never been recovered, and so on. I also think he formed a theory of his own about where the treasure was hidden."

"But surely he knew about Micklefield's expedition."

"Yes, of course. Still, he had his theory, and can't you see what it would have meant to him? He loathes farming, he told me that himself, but there didn't seem to be any way out."

"I can't believe—"

"Why else did he want to buy Brass Castle? It's unlikely that he wanted the responsibility for any more land, and some seventy-five acres of it had actually been his own until he sold them in 1940."

"There's that, of course," said Bill in unwilling agreement.

"So he bid against you at the sale, but his wife wouldn't back him—you told me that yourself, Bill—and so he was soon out of the running. That was in April. In May Mrs. Thornton had the first of a series of bilious attacks, probably quite genuine at that time, but when some months later he heard the rumor that you were in difficulties and thinking of selling again, they gave him an idea what to do."

"Do you suppose the rumor was current so long ago?" In spite of himself Bill was beginning to get interested.

"It's not really so long...August or September

when Margot Damerel brought Mrs. Thornton some homemade jam."

"You mean," said Jenny, "he decided to poison his wife and use her money to buy this place. And then, if he'd found the treasure he'd have kept it for himself."

"It would take some disposing of, but worth the trouble, don't you think?"

"If he's that sort of man," said Jenny, "I don't see why he never thought of that before...to kill her to get her money, I mean."

"Because it wasn't enough to retire on. He was taking a gamble, admittedly, but think what a difference it would have made to him...the difference between a few thousand pounds and a fortune. And as Hester doesn't sound to have been a very lovable person—"

"And he was probably already in love with Bess," said Bill in a hard voice.

"—there was nothing to stop him carrying out his plan."

"Except his conscience," said Jenny, with one of her unexpected retreats into primness.

"I can't possibly attempt to explain that, or his lack of it. But it must have seemed a good idea to him, and with very little risk involved. I imagine he got the shock of his life when Dr. Todd wouldn't sign the death certificate, but when he thought it out I expect he felt safe enough. It would be the devil and all to prove—"

"You're talking as if you know," Bill objected.

"I thought I made it clear that this is only a theory, and I only worked it out after Seth Dodgson was killed. Thornton was a friend of yours; I didn't want to think he was a murderer, though obviously it was the most likely answer. But at that stage, if I'd been the police, I think I should have tried asking Bob Clayton what he told Seth Dodgson on the

Tuesday afternoon. And also whether he heard the truck that came up the Edge last Saturday, and if it stopped at Stavethorpe.''

"What he told...this is getting very complicated," Jenny complained.

"Well, unless there's been an incredible coincidence—and I mean incredible—the two murders must be connected," said Antony. "There are two signposts here: Seth Dodgson told me when he called here on the Tuesday that he's also been to Stavethorpe Hall, and Thornton told me that Bob Clayton is a taciturn sort of chap, but for some reason always hung around for a word with Dodgson when opportunity offered. Putting those two things together, and granting that the second murder must have arisen out of the first, I would suggest that Bob saw something incriminating, which he told his friend Dodgson about, but not the police.''

"He might have seen Mr. Thornton pouring some of the wood preservative into a smaller, more convenient container," said Jenny. "It would have to be something like that—wouldn't it—something concrete, for him to notice at all.''

"You're probably right. I'll make a further guess and say that Dodgson and Thornton met in Great Allerton on the day of the inquest, which both of them attended, and that Dodgson made some guarded reference—without mentioning Bob Clayton—to what he knew. Thornton must have thought there was more to it than there really was...I can't see any jury convicting on young Clayton's evidence alone. Anyway, 'the guilty flee where no man pursueth.' There's no reason to suppose Dodgson was interested in blackmail, but his reputation as a gossip alone made him dangerous—''

"But Mr. Thornton had an alibi—" said Jenny again.

"Not if we assume that the black-market truck that stopped at Ferrenscross, according to Mrs. Dodgson's evidence, stopped also at Stavethorpe on its way there."

"That would mean that Cyril, as well as Seth Dodgson, was involved in the black market."

"Is there anything inherently unbelievable in that? He could have hopped in the back when they'd had their talk and Joe and Sidney were getting back into the cab again, and no one any the wiser. In fact, if we accept the evidence of the tire lever, that's what he must have done. There wasn't time for him to have walked both ways."

There was a pause. Antony retrieved his cup of cocoa and drank what was left of it, though by now it was nearly cold. Jenny was obviously thinking about what she had heard, but Bill...there was no telling what Bill was thinking. After a time he said, to Antony's surprise, "It's a good reconstruction. I wouldn't wonder if you were right." But he didn't sound as if he cared much one way or the other.

"What I'd like to know," said Jenny, "is where Mr. Thornton thought the treasure is hidden? If you're right about all this, of course."

"I've got an idea about that," said Antony. "It came to me tonight when we were talking about the way the old dairy is built. Suppose Hugh Ambler and his father buried the doings in the side of the hill, and then rebuilt the back wall in front of it. Everybody's always taken it for granted that the treasure was under the floor, but it needn't ever have been there at all."

Bill got to his feet. It looked to Antony as if every movement was an effort, and Jenny must have thought so, too, because she got up beside him and laid a hand on his arm. He looked down at her and said, more to her than to Antony, "If

you're interested, we shall know in the spring when
we trench around the back of the house."

"I don't think I can wait till then," said Jenny
frankly, and saw him smile for the first time that
evening.

"I don't see anything else for it. We can't do
anything until the snow has gone."

"It was only a thought, anyway," said Antony.
"An idea about an idea that somebody else might
have had. I don't suppose for a moment that there'll
be anything there to find."

# Epilogue

## April 1947

THEY STAYED ANOTHER MONTH at Brass Castle, and when Bill had dug out the car and saved enough petrol coupons to drive them the thirty-odd miles into Leeds to catch the train, the road was still only open as far as the top of Stavethorpe Edge and the countryside was even more deeply covered in snow. Bess had left the day after Cyril Thornton's arrest, apparently quite calm again; for all they could tell she might have forgotten her revelations of the evening before, but at the same time she took it for granted that her brief engagement to Bill was over. None of them had quite enough worldly wisdom to know how to deal with the situation except by ignoring it, which perhaps, in any case, was the best thing they could have done. And when Jenny got a letter from Bess only a fortnight later saying that she was staying in Rothershaw and was going to take a course in shorthand and typing, she left it unanswered for a little too long, and then replied in as few words as possible. Bill was still far too quiet when they said goodbye and got into the train for London, but to anyone who didn't know him well he would probably have seemed composed enough.

By the end of March the paint job was finished and they were able to move into their own quarters at the top of the house in Kempenfeldt Square. The living room was rather sparsely furnished, and still uncurtained, and Jenny was fully occupied looking for just the right material, and shopping for the other odd items that they hadn't been able to scrounge from either family. Antony was working diligently, and although he still had fits of restlessness they were growing fewer and farther between, and one way and another he was beginning to feel that the task he had set himself wasn't altogether beyond his capabilities.

One evening in late April they were having dinner with Sir Nicholas Harding, and afterward, over the coffee cups, were arguing in a rather desultory way whether the wing chairs from the morning room could be spared to grace the living room at the top of the house. Sir Nicholas was stretched out at his ease, watching with amused indulgence the effect of his arguments on Jenny, who was growing steadily more indignant. "I have told you, my dear, that you may have the chairs with my good will. But you must have the sofa, too."

"But, Uncle Nick, it's hideous. If you want to get rid of it—"

"I do."

"Well, then, why can't you send it to a rummage sale, or something?"

"It's much too comfortable. And when you're so badly in need of furniture—"

"We could manage with the two chairs, and get some others later."

"But how extravagant! I don't think I could reconcile it with my conscience—"

"Uncle Nick!"

"—though I might consider having it recovered, if that would help at all."

"It might," said Jenny. "It would still be hideous, of course, but at least we could get it done to match the chairs. What do you think, Antony?"

While they were talking, Antony had heard the front doorbell and had wandered out into the hall to pick up the late mail. He was coming back into the study as she spoke with some envelopes in his hand. "Three for you, Uncle Nick. They look like circulars. And one for us from Bill."

"How is he?" Jenny demanded.

"Give me a chance. Do you mind if I read it, sir? We're still a bit worried about Bill, you know."

"You may read it, of course," said Sir Nicholas. "Bill is not likely, however, to do anything foolish, and time—as too many people have said before me—is a great healer."

"But, Uncle Nick, he was quite horribly in love with Bess," said Jenny.

"I won't argue about that, though I don't altogether appreciate your choice of words." He broke off to glare at his nephew. "My dear boy, if you have something to communicate, say so. I am, after all, quite used to interruptions."

"I don't believe it," said Antony, almost stuttering in his excitement. "They've found the treasure."

"Where?" Perhaps nothing else could so immediately have diverted Jenny from her grievance about the sofa.

"In the hill behind the old dairy. As soon as the weather was right they started on the trench, and the walls fell down, just as Bill said they would, and had to be rebuilt and painted, but when they started on the back wall, right in the middle they found a chest... exactly like a storybook. And in it were all the things listed in Hugh Ambler's journal...jewels and gold plate and chalices and—" He put down the letter on his knee, and looked from one of them to the other. "I don't believe it," he said again.

"I hardly think, under the circumstances, that

Bill would be indulging his sense of humor at your expense."

"No, I don't think so, either. Bill doesn't seem a bit pleased about it. There'll be all sorts of legal carry-on, and it's his busy time of year; all the same, I bet the Damerels will be pretty bucked. But isn't it extraordinary, Uncle Nick?"

"If you will confine yourself to the English language," said Sir Nicholas austerely, "I will agree with anything you say."

"It's a long letter," Jenny pointed out. "You haven't read half of it yet."

"No. . . well. . . there's a lot about how the farm's doing; you'd better read that for yourself."

"Things are going well, I hope," said Sir Nicholas, who had known Bill for a long time and was more interested in his affairs than he would have cared to admit.

"Very well, from what he says. Huff and Puff have had their litters. . . twelve and ten. . . oh, and then he goes on about the trial."

"I suppose you mean Cyril Thornton. He was tried at the Spring Assizes at Arkenshaw. There was a report in the *Times*."

"Yes, but it just gave the verdict. . . that he was found guilty. No details of the evidence."

"Does Bill go into details?"

"No. He just says, 'It's surprising how accurate the summary you gave us was.' Well, he can't be more surprised than I am."

"The girl would have to give evidence, wouldn't she? Does he say anything about that?"

"I wouldn't expect him to. Nothing really sensational can have happened, or even the *Times* would have mentioned it."

"What I want to know more than anything else," said Jenny, "is how he is."

"You know Bill. There's no telling." He folded

the letter and put it back into its envelope again.
"If you want to know what I think, it'll be a long
time before he gets over Bess."

Jenny drank some of her coffee in a thoughtful
way. "I liked her, you know . . . I really did, before I
knew. But now I think the country people weren't
so very far wrong in what they were saying."

"Of course they weren't. I don't know whether
she and Thornton were lovers or not, though I'd
rather think they were."

"Why?"

"Because it makes her getting engaged to Bill
more logical. Anyway, she was certainly in love
with Thornton."

"I know that; it's obvious. I meant that they were
right in the rest of what they said . . . about her being a witch. No, really, I mean it," she added, as
both the men—for once in agreement—began to
protest at this unreasonable statement. "She 'overlooked' Hester Thornton—isn't that what they call
it—and the poor woman started having bilious attacks. And that was what gave Mr. Thornton the
idea . . . you said that yourself, Antony—"

But both Antony and Sir Nicholas, talking together, were already trying to convince her of the
error of her ways.

*Be a detective.*
*See if you can solve . . .*

# Raven House
## MINUTE
## MYSTERY #3

On the following page is Raven House
MINUTE MYSTERY #3, "Alibi."

Every month each Raven House book will feature a
MINUTE MYSTERY, a unique little puzzler designed
to let *you* do the sleuthing!

U.S. (except Arizona) residents may check their
answer by calling **1-800-528-1404** during the
months of January and February 1982. U.S. residents
may also obtain the solution by writing anytime
during or after this period to:

Raven House MINUTE MYSTERY
1440 South Priest Drive
Tempe, AZ 85281

Canadian residents, please write to the following
address:

Raven House MINUTE MYSTERY
649 Ontario Street
Stratford, Ontario N5A 6W2

# ALIBI

The professor was in an expansive mood.

"I've often observed," he told his dinner guests, "how extremely difficult it is to fake an unassisted alibi. The recent Werner affair in Chicago is a case in point."

He fired a cigar and continued. "I had no suspicion of Werner when I bumped into him on Michigan Avenue the morning after a friend of his had been found murdered. When I casually inquired where he'd been between four and six o'clock the previous afternoon, he gave the following account.

" 'It was such a glorious afternoon that about two o'clock I went for a sail. When I was about eight miles offshore—about 5:30—the wind died down completely. There wasn't a breath of air. Drifting about I recalled that the international distress signal is a flag flown upside down, so I ran mine to the top of the mast in that manner and waited in the dead calm.

" 'Shortly after six o'clock the freighter, *Luella*, heaved to, and I went aboard her after securing my boat with a towline. Her skipper said he'd seen my distress signal about three miles away. He put me ashore at Harvey's Landing, and a passing car gave me a lift to town. Imagine my surprise when I read in the morning paper that the *Luella* had sunk in a storm last night and all hands had been lost!' "

The professor sipped his wine and went on. "While the *Luella* had been sunk with loss of entire crew, I immediately arrested Werner for further questioning. I knew his alibi was faked."

*How did the professor know?*

From **Minute Mysteries** by Austin Ripley.
Copyright © 1949 by Opera Mundi, Paris.

# ℛaven House Mysteries

## An exciting opportunity to read some of the finest in mystery fiction!

As a Raven House subscriber you will receive every month 4 action-filled, spine-chilling mystery novels, superbly written by talented authors who are all members of the prestigious MYSTERY WRITERS OF AMERICA.
*You may cancel your subscription whenever you wish.*
Should you decide to stop your order, just let us know and we'll cancel all further shipments.

*COMPLETE AND MAIL THIS COUPON TODAY!*